Nunca uma dedicatória fez tanto sentido.

Estou lançando meu primeiro livro no mesmo mês.

E se não fosse por todo o acolhimento de vocês, isso nunca teria acontecido.

Do fundo do coração,

Obrigado!!

Rythm Of Death

A tale of crime, music and purpose

Arnaldo Neto

Arnaldo Neto
Londres,
15.03.24

To my father, who enabled me to dream.

To my mother, who taught me how to make others dream.

To Gabi, my dream come true.

Past

The boy barely slept that night.

As soon as the sun came up, he jumped out of his bed, ran into the room beside his and threw himself into his parents' bed.

More specifically, on his father's neck.

> "Wake up, Dad! It's time!"
>
> "I'm coming, son", said the man, still half asleep but smiling. "I'm coming… I'm coming…".

They were about to hit the road on yet another road trip.

Starting point: London.

Destination: The Scottish Highlands.

Soundtrack: *Save Me* by Fleetwood Mac.

Present

I'm in the dressing room. I've already finished warming up my voice. The instruments are tuned. I can hear the roar of the screaming fans from here. In a few minutes, I will be singing all our hits with each and every one of them.

Suddenly, a drop of cold sweat trickles down my back. My heart starts pounding so hard that it seems it might pop out of my chest. My hands tremble. I run to the bathroom. The vomit almost tears open my throat. I can't breathe. I think I'm going to die. Help!

My cry for help is what finally wakes me up from my nightmare.

Monday, 8:00 a.m. in London.

Waking up at this hour may not seem too early by your standards, but it's certainly a victory for someone who, until recently, would stay up all night and sleep all day.

I open my eyes.

Even though I quit smoking a little while ago, the craving for a cigarette still echoes in my mouth.

Prologue

The figure positions the unconscious body with its back against the wall.

While the exterior of the location is bucolic, the interior is dark.

Almost as much as what is about to happen in minutes.

The man about to be executed begins to regain consciousness.

In flashes of lucidity, he glimpses disconnected elements.

A monster.

A vinyl record.

The shadow approaches.

Grabs the subject by the neck.

Strangulation?

An amateur technique.

The masked villain opens the poor fellow's throat wide.

And with a perfect movement, makes a cut at the spot with the circular artefact.

Blood splatters.

The victim's last gasps of life are filled with the first chords of a familiar melody.

Until everything turns into darkness.

10:18 a.m. - BBC London newspaper:

"The UK's rejoining the EU? You heard that right. The Prime Minister's latest measures indicate the possibility of…"

"Come again?"

"This just in…"

"A man was found dead in an abandoned building near Regents Park. The 62-year-old victim, William Gardner, was found with his throat slashed - apparently by a vinyl record, which was playing at the crime scene covered in blood."

"Warning, some viewers may find the following scenes disturbing…"

Side A

Intro

That's why I try to fight the temptation by engaging in much healthier habits like exercising.

Yesterday was abs day. Today, it's push-ups. But not before putting on my meticulously thought-out playlist.

That's right, I have a soundtrack for everything you can imagine: driving, travel, sleeping, self-reflection, sex... And my one for training starts with *Positive Tension* by Bloc Party.

As you can see, I am so passionate about rock that I started talking about music even before introducing myself.

Nice to meet you, I'm David June, or as my friends call me, DJ - both because of my initials and because of my mania for having background music on for every moment of my life, just like I'm doing now.

I work out for around 30 minutes and finish my training exactly when my playlist gets to *Killing In The Name* by Rage Against the Machine, which means that it's time for the hardest part of my morning ritual: an ice-cold shower.

It's June, late springtime in England, but the weather hasn't started warming up yet. After a surprising week of high temperatures at the end of May, the sixth month of the year started with temperatures averaging 10 degrees and rain. A snapshot of the city with one of the most dynamic climates in the world.

But if it's freezing out there, having a recently-stimulated body will make my mission easier. Let's get on with it.

Shower taken.

On the way from the bathroom to my room, I stop and look at myself in the hallway mirror. Today I turn 33, but I don't see many reasons why I should celebrate this.

I still see a boy. Maybe it's because I'm far from achieving what I thought I would at this stage in my life. In some ways, I feel like a failure.

With this line of thought weighing me down, the next step of my morning ritual makes perfect sense: meditation.

At first, I'd considered this step even more challenging than the cold shower. Just sitting in silence and closing my eyes was enough for my mind to start flooding with ideas, melodies and lyrics for new compositions rather than being in tranquillity.

But now, after a few months of practice and with the help of guided audio sessions, I am already able to calm my mind for at least ten minutes.

With one more deep breath, I'm finally ready to take on the day.

And what about breakfast, you might be wondering?

I still drool over the thought of eggs, bacon and sausage, but as per the doctor's order, I've been subject to cruel intermittent fasting to help balance my cholesterol levels - which used to be higher than the volume in my headphones.

At face value, it may even seem like I'm a role model. Practically an urban monk. But the truth is, all this is more due to necessity rather than to strong discipline.

When I was 17 years old, I started a band called "The Sunflowers" with a few of my friends.

We weren't a huge hit, but my musical career was the excuse I needed to adopt the worst habits of an aspiring rock star: drinking, smoking, all-nighters and fast food.

After 10 years of this, I gave up on my dream of saving lives through music to save my own.

An alarming blood test result, my mum's dismissal and some emotional baggage that I'm not quite ready to unpack yet, all made me give up the stage and change my lifestyle.

And yes, you read that right, I said that my dream was to save people through music.

It may sound pretentious, but I deeply believe that we inhabit this planet to share the gifts the world gives us with the people around us.

The name of my band embodies this idea. The Sunflowers, named after the flower that absorbs light from our star when it's sunny. And shares its energy with other flowers on rainy days.

The dynamic is an excellent metaphor for what we wanted to achieve as a group. Share our musical gifts with the world and inspire crowds with our chords and lyrics.

Have I still not convinced you of the power of bass, guitar, and drums? Perhaps a personal example would do the trick.

Music saved my life. I'm not kidding. I remember exactly when.

Everything I did felt pointless, nothing inspired me, until one day in December 2000, my father called me over.

"Son, listen to this..."

It was the first notes of *Beautiful Day* by U2.

The heart-like beats of the drum seemed to keep up with the beats of my own - which had never beaten so hard, by the way.

That's when everything changed. I became a total rock n' roll addict.

Composing, playing and singing it.

The songs gave me direction. Meaning. Purpose. And if the combination of voice and instruments did so much for me, I also wanted to be a messenger and give the same experience to others. I wanted to pay that magic forward.

I was born to do this, I feel it in my bones. I am moved when I do it.

When I used to do it.

When we get to know each other a bit better, I'll tell you the reasons why I stepped away from it all.

I haven't completely abandoned my mission and greatest love, but, instead of inspiring thousands on stage like I imagined I would, now I work at the Rough Trade, a vinyl store where I earn enough to help out at home while still being able to listen to my heroes all day long. In addition to getting many free tickets to concerts.

My work is a cowardly attempt of still being in touch with my passion. Like a man head over heels, pretending to be someone else for some girl online.

That's where I'm heading now.

I leave my house on King's Cross at 9:15 a.m.

I live in a flat near my district's Underground station. Leaving the station, continue up Euston Road for 10 minutes and we're here.

I share it with my mum and we share practically a big room with a kitchenette and a bathroom. We improvised a curtain divider between her space and the "living room" where I sleep on the couch.

I've already lost count of how many times she barged into my corner, furious about how loud the radio was.

I haven't been worried about this over the past few days because she's in Scotland, visiting my grandmother in a small town in Galloway. I would have loved to go with her, even more so by car, driving down the beautiful roads of our neighbouring country, but unfortunately, I couldn't get the time off work.

The good news is, I have the whole house to myself and I can make as much noise as I want.

My mum's name is Dolores and she has a big heart. I never imagined that I'd still be living with her at this point in my life, but she's too good of a person, which makes it easier to live together. Imagine a mix between Princess Diana and Audrey Hepburn. Her face is more similar to Audrey's, but her hair reminds me of Lady Di. Then, add in some of Mother Teresa's kindness. That's the woman who brought me into the world.

And if I spend another minute describing her, I am going to be overwhelmed by my emotions and miss work. It's time to hit the road.

According to my previous times, it takes me forty-five minutes to walk to work.

The walks, which were also recommended by my doctor, were another way to introduce exercise into my formerly sedentary routine. That's why I'll be wearing my trainers instead of leather boots.

In my ears, headphones. To listen to rock star biography audiobooks.

Reading has always been a thorn in my side, but being able to listen to books while I walk solved this problem. Today I'm starting my commute with *Born To Run*, Bruce Springsteen's biography.

You know, I identify a lot with Springsteen. Whether it be for his Irish descent or because both of us are the eldest grandson of a large family that fell apart. Springsteen's lyrics always spoke to me, full of dreams and promises of a life of grandeur.

Learning about his story and idealising my own made the walk fly by. Not as quickly as it would with my motorbike, Triumph Bobber, that's true, but right now she's parked away in the garage.

Anything for good health.

I already told you about my love for bands like Bloc Party, Bruce Springsteen, and Rage Against the Machine. I even explained the origin of my band's name, but I have yet to explain my own, which has to do with good old rock.

My late father was completely obsessed with U2 and Queen. He took inspiration from U2 for the name David - not many people know this, but Bono Vox's real name is Paul David Hewson - and June comes from Queen.

Any sort of allusion to Freddie Mercury would be too obvious, so my old man preferred to honour the guitarist, Brian May. Since *June* is the month after *May* and is also the month I was born, the choice was obvious.

David June! A name fit for a star, right?

My head's in the clouds, but in order to arrive at the store punctually at 10, I come back down to earth and remind myself that my life of concerts is behind me.

I work in Notting Hill. You've probably already heard of the neighbourhood because of the film featuring Hugh Grant and Julia Roberts, but, for me, what makes working in this historical area even cooler is what happens on the street perpendicular to where I work.

The Portobello Road Market is a mix of food stands and second-hand stores. This is where I buy my vinyl records and my clothes, and where I sample a wide variety of delicacies. Saturday is the best day to visit the market because the shops are set up on the sidewalks flooded with both Londoners and tourists.

I'll never forget the last birthday I celebrated there. A few friends and I spent the day discovering vinyls, clothes and flavours. The result: a leather jacket in the best '70s rock star style, a mint condition vinyl record of *Exile on Main Street* by the Rolling Stones, and meal I'll never forget that mixed the best of the brazilian, jamaican and french cuisines.

As you can see, I have an exceptional memory. I can remember every detail of meals, concerts, and films. My friends joke that it's my superpower and they love to test my memory capacity through challenges, ones that I usually overcome with ease.

This very ability takes me away from the present for a few moments, allowing me to taste yet again the rich flavours I just described.

Until a customer enters the store, snapping me out of my daydream.

Who knows, maybe this weekend I'll reacquaint myself with these tastes? But today's another day on the grind. Another ordinary day, only varying slightly by regulars wishing me happy birthday.

You know what I wanted for my birthday? For time to go faster.

If only.

In fact, thinking about it only makes the minutes drag on, that's why I'm going to go clean up some of the classic records in hopes that it'll lift my spirits.

Let's go with Pink Floyd, it's always a best-seller.

While dusting off *The Wall*, I put on *Dark Side Of The Moon*, but here comes my co-worker, Pamela to turn on the TV.

I hate when someone throws off my ambient music with unnecessary noise, but Pamela and her constant bad attitude are specialists at making me want to pull my hair out.

Today, her usual stone-cold expression is struck with shock.

She walks around the counter, walks up to me and says:

"David, you gotta see this."

Future

In the dressing room, the young man prepares to go on stage.

Visualisation. Meditation. Respiration. All so that the paralysing anxiety from years ago doesn't re-emerge tonight.

Today, more than ever, it can't happen again.

More than 100,000 crazed fans at the Glasgow Summer Sessions await him in the audience.

> "Good evening, Scotland!", says the singer, his lips resting against the microphone, "tonight we're going to start with a cover."

To the audience's delight, he strums the first chords of *Save Me* by Fleetwood Mac.

Side A

Track 1

"Hey you

The one with laughing eyes

You, the one with the haunting stare

Well you

You have the power to hypnotise

I should'a known better

I should beware..."

Save Me - Fleetwood Mac

Past

The father tiptoes over to the boy's bed.

A smile spreads across his face as he silently approaches him and strokes his brown hair.

"Hey, this time, I'm the one waking you up", he teases.

The young boy opens his eyes, which match his locks, and smiles back at him.

"I knew you'd come before the sun came up, Dad. You've always loved the roads here."

At 6 in the morning, the pair head to breakfast in their small inn in the Irish countryside.

Faced with the uncertainty of when their next meal would be, they devour all the eggs, bacon and everything they're entitled to.

After all, the day was dedicated to exploring the heart of the country in yet another long car ride.

Soundtrack: *Belfast Child* by Simple Minds.

Present

The news being covered on every channel is bizarre. Almost unbelievable.

When I hear it, I drop the disk that I'm cleaning.

David Gilmour, Roger Waters, and Co. deserve better treatment but I suddenly feel dirty, as if I'm holding the murder weapon.

A man in his 60s was found dead with his throat slit open. And do you know what the instrument of crime was? A vinyl record, exactly like the ones that surround me every day.

I move closer to the TV so I can hear the news better.

The media has nicknamed the murderer the *Psycho Killer*, as a reference to one of the Talking Heads' classic hits, who had left the weapon covered in blood, playing on a perfectly preserved record player at the crime scene.

The choice of album, *Behind the Mask* by Fleetwood Mac was already quite suggestive, but not as much as the song that was left playing: *Save Me*, the album's 5th track.

An intense feeling washes over me, a strange attraction to the scene.

Don't get me wrong, what happened was horrific, but I can't help but think of the attention to detail that the killer had with his choice of music…and even his equipment.

I think it's strange that no one else has noticed or commented on it.

With these strange ideas floating around in my head and *Save Me* playing on repeat in the back of my mind, the hours of my workday fly by, until it's time for me to head home.

I arrive at home at my usual time, around 7:00 p.m. I look at my guitar. She looks back at me. Memories of the day that changed everything flash before my eyes.

Remember when I told you about my band, "The Sunflowers"?

Well, I didn't mention that we were relatively well-known in London's alternative scene. So well, in fact, that after a few pub and party gigs, we were invited to play at the famous Glastonbury Festival, the very same that helped Coldplay and Radiohead rise to fame.

It still pains me to talk about it.

All I can tell you now is that, on the day that we could have become real rock stars, I had a panic attack and was unable to perform. I went to the festival, warmed up and, with only a few hours left before going up on stage, I ran away like a little boy afraid of the dark.

Since then, I can't bring myself to play.

My instruments are hung up like decorations and are only good for taking up space in our already cramped apartment.

But today, something inside me is different.

I feel an indescribable urge to play.

Which song?

The very same that was left playing at one of the most horrific murders in recent London history.

I feel somewhat guilty, but I can't hold myself back.

I ignore the happy birthday messages from my friends and disregard any invitations to celebrate. Instead of tuning in to them, I tune my Fender Stratocaster's strings.

A mix of feelings washes over me as the first notes echo through the room.

Feeling both ecstatic to discover that I've still got it, and deeply disturbed that I'm performing the soundtrack of today's gruesome event.

Despite my discomfort, I go with the flow.

Practically playing Fleetwood Mac all night long.

Only stopping when I finally fall asleep holding my guitar.

Future

No white roses, organic cotton towels or volcanic water.

Backstage, the only thing the young man asked for was a yoga mat for his stretches and meditation. A limber body will make all the difference in the challenge that's about to commence.

That's giving more than 50,000 hysterical fans at Belfast's Victoria Park what they came to see: an epic night of rock.

> "Good evening, Ireland! Today we're going to start out a bit differently, with a song that I hope means as much to you as it does to me…"

All alone up on stage, the singer starts singing a cappella the Irish anthem, *Belfast Child* by Simple Minds.

The audience joins in to sing along.

Side A

Track 2

"The streets are empty

Life goes on.

One day we'll return here

When the Belfast Child sings again"

Belfast Child - Simple Minds

Past

"Wake up, sleepy head!"

Hearing his father's voice, the boy stretches himself awake in the car's back seat.

"The night went by so fast. Feels like I barely slept."

The little boy sits up in his seat, still drowsy, and looks out the window.

"Wow, it's still dark."

And it really was. The man had started driving at around 5 in the morning, with his son in the back seat. Everything was planned for catching the sunrise in the bucolic outskirts of Cambridge.

"Today's trip is going to be different, son", he answers without taking his eyes off the road, "and to make sure that we stay wide awake, the path to get there is about to get more exciting…"

He takes one hand off the wheel to turn up the radio.

Soundtrack: *Killer* by Adamski.

Present

The day starts at a snail's pace.

The few hours I've slept don't help either.

Getting back into playing reminds me of all the dreams I gave up on and forces me to confront who I could have become.

In the life that I left behind.

On the other hand, I'm playing pretty damn well, I'd even say the best I've played in a while.

It's just a shame that what got the ball rolling again was the song playing at the event that shocked all of London.

In an attempt to try to disassociate myself from the *Psycho Killer*, I play around with the notes. I throw together a few chords and surprise myself with my crafted melody. This could be my first composition in years.

The idea excites me.

Enveloped in a mix of ecstasy and guilt, I get ready for another day at work.

Motivated by this morning's epiphany, I kick open the *Rough Trade*'s door like an American cowboy.

I need some music that expresses how I'm feeling.

I turn on the TV and search *Celebration Day* on YouTube.

Never heard of it?

I'm talking about a film that Led Zeppelin recorded during a historic show at the O2 Arena in 2007, right here in London.

Packed with a setlist including songs like *Black Dog*, *A Whole Lotta Love*, *Rock and Roll*, and other hit songs, I start cleaning up my favourite vinyl section: the classics.

That's when, yet again, Pamela ruins the moment by switching to the news channel.

I open my mouth to complain when suddenly I see something on the screen that renders me speechless.

He's back.

Another murder. Exactly one day later. With the same *modus operandi*.

And once again, I was holding the murder weapon: a record.

At first, I thought it was a rerun of yesterday's news, but no.

There's a new song playing on the record player, another vinyl covered in blood.

And if *Save Me* by Fleetwood Mac had stirred up some buried emotions, this one was a punch in the stomach.

It's *Belfast Child* from the band Simple Minds. Track 9 from the album *Street Fighting Years*…my favourite one at that.

My late father was born in Belfast, the capital of Northern Ireland. And I, as his son, am literally a "Belfast Child".

Hearing of the first crime, I was able to mask my feeling of terror and admiration for the criminal, this time, I couldn't.

I tell Pamela that I'm not feeling well and run home.

When I get to my room, I see my guitar practically begging me:

"Pick me up, touch me."

Like a man possessed by the empowerment of playing his guitar, I start belting out the accompaniment of yet another horrendous crime.

I feel like I'm back up on stage.

I shiver runs up my spine.

How could I have given this up?

I play *Save Me* and *Belfast Child* back to back, practically throwing a tribute concert to the *Psycho Killer*. I can't help but think about what all this means.

I feel a strange connection with the killer, particularly with his song choices.

Could it be that he understands rock as well as I do? Perhaps more than I do?

My good, old competitive side comes out.

I need to prove to myself that nobody knows these artists as well as I do.

By playing the singles dozens of times in a row, I can not only reproduce them perfectly.

But I also feel a connection. I cry out enthusiastically.

> "These songs are connected!"

Future

It's time for the encore during an intimate show at the Q Club, one of the few remaining Cambridge nightclubs.

It will be the first time that the young man, now accustomed to crowded stadiums, will perform in one.

Usually, he starts his final sequence of songs with a slow ballad, but this ambience calls for something a little more lively…

> "Let's see who remembers this one. Sing with me."

In perfect harmony with the house DJ, he starts playing a rock remix of *Killer* by Adamski.

Side A

Track 3

"So you want

To be free?

To live your life

The way you wanna be

Will you give

If we cry?

Will we live

Or will we die?"

Killer - Adamski

Past

  "Ohh… Heaven is a place on Earth", sings the boy, full of energy. "Wake up, dad!"

The father jumps out of bed, scared out of his wits.

  "What time is it?", he asks.

  "I don't know, it's still dark…"

The man checks the time on his watch resting on the nightstand.

  "Two in the morning." "Go to sleep, young man." Tomorrow's your choir's performance day.

  "I know, but I can't", answers the boy, "I'm too excited!"

Giving in, the parent gets up and gets ready.

A short time later, the duo is settled into the car. The driver checks on his son in the back seat who is properly fastened in his seat belt.

Soundtrack: *Heaven Is A Place On Earth* by Belinda Carlisle.

It only took the first few verses to get the boy to start feeling sleepy.

On restless nights, the roar of the motor combined with music was the perfect sleeping ritual to calm him down.

Present

By playing the hits that the Psycho Killer used in his crimes back to back, I remember that I used to listen to them in this exact order.

They were the first two songs on my dad's CD called *Hot 88*, featuring the biggest hits in my birth year.

The first two tracks are connected. I'm sure of it.

Upon discovering this, questions start to uncontrollably pop into my mind.

Will there be a third victim and a third song?

Can I piece together which song it will be?

And is it possible that, from this information, I will be able to predict the next murder?

If I'm capable of doing this, I could even prevent the crimes.

This wasn't how I had imagined that I'd save lives through music, but suddenly I feel important again.

Just as when I would go up on stage and the audience would chant my name.

That's what gives me meaning.

Oh, how I missed this feeling.

Doing something with purpose. Not being just another ordinary guy, living a boring, average life.

I matter. I can be useful.

I run to my records shelf and start sifting through my collection. There's a link between these songs, I just need to find out what it is.

I sit on the ground with several vinyl covers, CDs, and DVDs scattered around me. My eyes run along each one.

My mind's on fire.

I always had an enviable ability to recall facts, especially when it comes to music.

I'm the guy who tells you all the songs from all the U2 albums, in order.

I know all their songs by heart.

I can also tell you the complete setlists of the more than one hundred shows I've been to.

My ability to recall every sound and memory I've ever experienced is definitely one of my strongest skills.

To finally be able to use this for good is extremely satisfying.

I put my head to work with all the willpower I can muster.

Think, David, think.

I try to find a connection between the songs and the crimes. Think of rhythms, street names, festivals, dates…

Dates.

For a brief moment, my heart seems to stop. Something tells me that I'm on to something.

I concentrate on recalling the release dates of each song but give in to my frustration.

They don't line up.

But what if it wasn't the release date? What if…

My eyes widen when it hits me.

My stomach churns and a bitter taste surges in my mouth. I almost throw up.

Save Me topped countless English radio music charts on the same day of the first murder, except in the year 1988.

The same goes for *Belfast Son*, which was also featured on June 2nd of that year.

That's it. The Psycho Killer chooses his tainted records based on the number-one hits on the most-played song lists in June 1988.

He's going to kill again and his song of choice will be the one that topped the charts on the 3rd day of June.

Which one was it?

I get up and walk around the room, softly tapping my head in hopes of giving my brain a boost.

June 3rd, David, June 3rd, June 3rd, June 3rd…

Suddenly, I stop in my tracks.

Killer, I recall. *The top song on June 3rd, 1988 was Killer by Adamski featuring Seal.*

I run over to the phone.

> "Hello, is this Scotland Yard? I know when the Psycho Killer will strike again."

I'm transferred back and forth a few times, giving my name, and my contact information. Each time I explain that no, this is not a prank call until I finally speak with a detective.

I explain everything I just pieced together. How the songs are connected to June, 1988. How they were the most played songs on the radio. I end my statement declaring with all the certainty in the world that the Psycho Killer is going to strike again.

As soon as the words come out of my mouth, I puff up my chest in pride. A rare sight to see over these past few years.

But when reality hits me, I feel like I've run straight into a concrete wall.

> "My boy, I appreciate the effort, but none of this is useful to me", states the detective on the other side of the line.
>
> "I-I'm sorry?", is all I could muster.
>
> "We're not cavemen. A quick search on Wikipedia was all it took for us to understand the killer's *modus operandi*. We've been on high alert since this morning."

Silence.

What in the world was I thinking? Obviously, they already know about all this. They're trained investigators who have access to a huge database. They're way more fit for the job than I am.

The detective breaks the silence with a polite but firm request to end the call:

> "If you find any more information about where the killer will commit his next crime, please give us another call. Have a good night."

A heavy weariness consumes me.

Did you really believe that these murders were connected to you in some way?, I think to myself. *That these songs were put on for me to hear and ultimately to catch the killer?*

I sit on the living room couch and rest my head in my hands.

Who do you think you are, David June?

I need to face the fact that, since I stopped doing shows, I feel empty inside. As if I never found my place in this world.

My purpose has always been to save lives through music. It's what I always tried to do every time I picked up a guitar. But yet again, I've fallen into the traps set by my own ego.

I had already resigned myself to being just another guy who likes music. Another face in the crowd, amidst the audience, and not the one on stage. But, from what I can tell, deep down inside I still cling to the hope of doing something grand.

I chuckle at the ridiculous role I played.

I was desperate enough to fabricate this huge fantasy involving two deaths. Of two hateful acts.

I'm such a pretentious asshole.

At this moment, I feel crushed by everything around me.

By my half-assed job. By still living with my mother. By my vanity and cowardice.

I feel so small. Weak.

I promised you that I wouldn't go back to my old habits, but right now I need them all.

Just to feel a little less like trash, even if it's just to fool myself for a little while.

I run to my wardrobe. I throw my runners across the room and put on my brown boots. Next comes my leather jacket and I head to the garage.

There she is, waiting for me. My motorbike, Triumph Bobber, that I vowed to sell after a drunk driving fall. I haven't taken her out for a ride in months. It's time. I just need to do one thing first: fuel up.

Not for my motorbike, she's already at full tank. For me.

My fuel's called nicotine.

I pick up the pack of Marlboros that I left stored inside my helmet, which rests on my bike's seat. I pull out a cigarette. Light it. The soft crackle of a lit cigarette is enough to make me shiver. I take a drag, keep the cigarette in my mouth, put on my helmet and take off down the streets of London, towards my favourite pub.

I haven't had a drink in a long time, so trying an Irish Red Ale was practically orgasmic.

I allow myself to indulge in several of them…for hours on end.

I drag myself home. I flop face-down on the couch with my boots still firmly tied to my feet.

My head spins, lulled by the alcohol, song ideas, and a throbbing pain. In the midst of all my scrambled thoughts, I remember a part of my conversation with Scotland Yard.

If you find any more information about where the killer will commit his next crime, please give us another call. Have a good night.

You know, they didn't dismiss me completely. If I had any lead on where the next crime is going to be or who the next victim will be, I could have a real shot at helping out.

Now my thoughts are locked in an intense internal battle.

While half of my mind is racing, rationalising how to find the location of the third crime, the other half tells me that I'm a spoiled brat who thinks he's special and should completely forget about all of this.

It's already broken into early morning on Wednesday, June 3rd and the aftermath of my excessive behaviour keeps me humble. I'm hungover and exhausted, and above all, I need to sober up before my shift starts in a few hours.

I should sleep out of respect for the job that helps me pay the bills, but I have a shot at taking down the Psycho Killer. This speaks louder to me.

A stream of energy courses through me. I jump up off the couch, grab a pen and paper and start up my laptop.

I need to know if the songs that were left playing at the crime scenes give any clues as to where the next murders could take place. Our about who will be targeted.

I combine my knowledge and my search results, furiously jotting down everything I consider relevant about *Save Me*.

My first instinct is to find a connection between the songs and the location of the crime.

I recall that the first victim was found in an abandoned building near Regents Park.

I look for some sort of connection online, but nothing jumps out at me. Instead, the results show lots of unreliable information, confusing articles, and sites trying to sell me something.

Annoyed, I close my browser and retreat to my memories.

Google, Wikipedia or artificial intelligence won't be any help in solving this one.

It's up to me.

My pounding headache doesn't help, but through meditation, I'm able to calm my whirlwind of thoughts.

And then, I remember.

On one of the road trips with my dad, we were listening to *Save Me* when he told me a fun fact.

The first time this song had ever been performed live was at a show. A performance in Regents Park.

My heart starts racing.

Could that be it? Let's see if I come to the same conclusion with the second crime.

The second crime happened in an empty lot close to Richmond Park, London's largest biking route.

Is there really a connection between such a peaceful place and Belfast Child?

I close my eyes and sift through my extensive yet scattered collection of memories. What immediately comes to mind is a story from Rolling Stone magazine.

Written in it, is the answer.

Belfast Son was indeed first shown to the public in that bicycle jungle during a Simple Minds acoustic show.

Oh my god! Could this be the pattern?

Abandoned lots and buildings near the places where the songs were performed live for the first time?

If that's the answer, I need to find out where the general public heard the hit single, *Killer*, for the first time.

My previous frustrating experience with internet searches make me only consider consulting it again.

I run to check my records. I take one by Adamsky and put it on. I listen to *Killer* in an obsessive loop.

I know this song. Memories meld in my mind.

Of my childhood. Of walking around the area. Of taking the Underground.

I remember an exhibition that was held in the station's tunnels.

With posters of the shows taking place nearby.

In a trance, I walk around my house, recreating the steps I took back then, admiring the snapshots of my favourite artists.

In my mind, I reach the end of the tunnel.

And I find what I was looking for.

An incredible action shot of Ademski screaming *Killer*'s chorus

The song premiered in 1988 in an intimate performance, just outside the station.

Will the next victim be found just a few metres from where I am?

I glance at the clock. It's 3:57 a.m. The murders happen at 4 in the morning.

I have 3 minutes.

My first thought is to call Scotland Yard, but even if I were able to convince them, they'd never make it in time.

What should I do?

I've barely slept, I'm still feeling the effects of all the beer I drank, and there's the possibility that I might run into a killer.

Screw it.

I throw on my leather jacket and mount my motorbike.

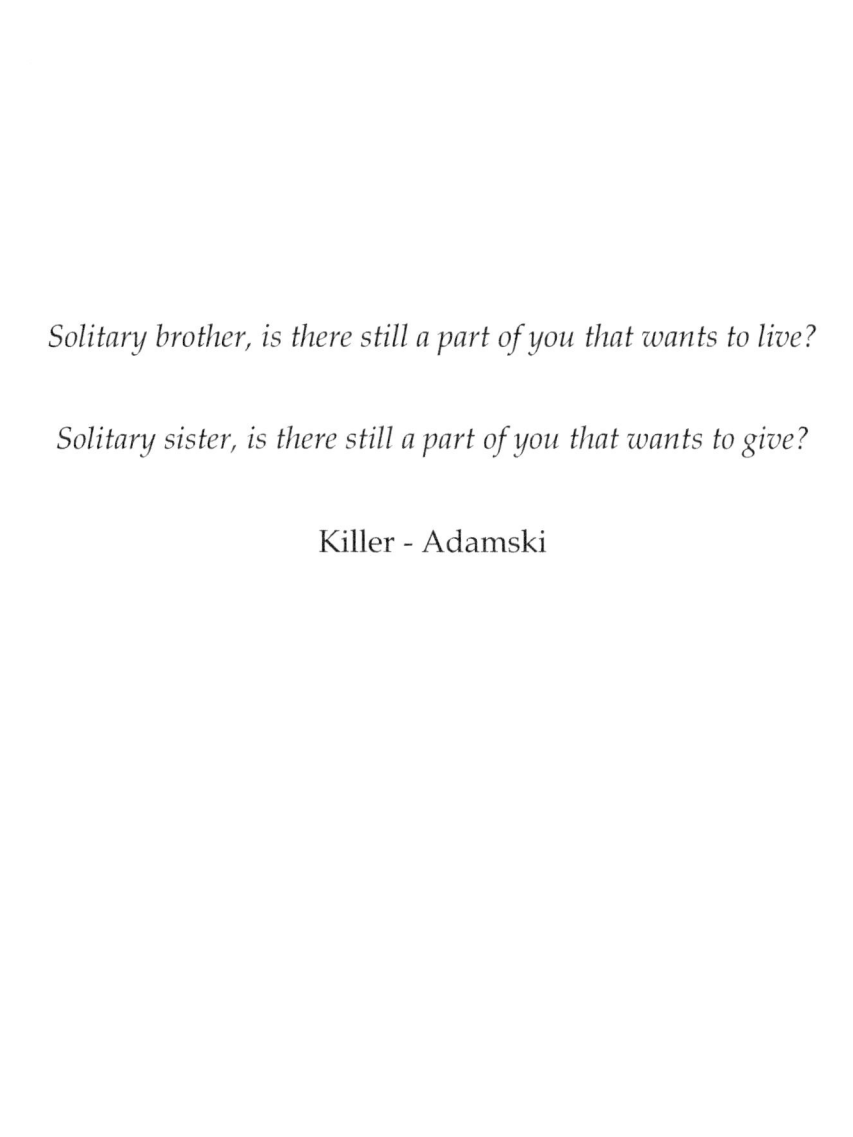

Solitary brother, is there still a part of you that wants to live?

Solitary sister, is there still a part of you that wants to give?

Killer - Adamski

King's Cross station is a 15-minute walk from my flat.

By bike, I'll be there in 2.

But now what?

How will I find something like an abandoned house this pitch-black, brisk London morning?

I try to piece together a mental map with my memories of the area.

My already pristine memory seems like it's on steroids with the recent source of stimuli.

Remembering everything like this is a blessing.

But also a curse.

I can recall that Bono sang a part of "Songbird" by the Beatles at the end of the Beautiful Day in the show that he did at the O2 Arena in 2017.

But I also recall every instance of bullying that I suffered from in my childhood.

Who told me to not interact with my peers and instead spent my entire recess listening to music?

Taking advantage of my gift, I reminisce about my childhood.

About my stage debut. About my father, standing there in the middle of the crowd.

At the time, I was singing in a small church choir nearby.

There's absolutely no way the Psycho Killer would know about this, but I trust my gut.

I drive there on autopilot, as if I hadn't gone almost 30 years without setting foot in that once-sacred place.

Nowadays?

I don't see anything sacred about this place.

Time transformed this quaint church into an abandoned one, the air tense like in a horror movie. I don't have time to be afraid. It's already 4 in the morning.

I kick down the door and enter the space where I discovered my talent for singing. The feeling is so majestic that it seems like I can hear myself chant the chorus of *Heaven Is A Place On Earth* by Belinda Carlisle - the same song that I sang in this very room on that distant day in my childhood. The chords echo so clearly in my mind that it seems like the music is actually playing.

I approach the central courtyard. It was there where I projected my voice for the world to hear for the first time and received applause in return.

The music grows louder, except it's not *Heaven Is A Place On Earth* anymore.

It's *Killer* by Adamski.

My mind returns from its trip down memory lane. I'm not hallucinating from the beer or lack of sleep. This is really happening.

It gets to the chorus and every line screams at me.

The song leads me through the dark. There's no doubt about it, the song is playing somewhere inside here.

I turn my phone's flashlight and unfortunately, I find out where.

From a record player. In mint condition. And the disk's covered in blood.

I'm at the crime scene.

I shine my light around the room and that's when I see it. A body. A throat. Cut open.

My egocentric saviour-of-the-world fantasies hadn't prepared me for the reality of the situation.

When reports about crimes like this are on TV, I'm always shocked by humanity's cruelty, but nothing compares to seeing it first-hand.

The body wasn't just a name on the news. Nor was he a number in a study or statistic.

He was a person. Someone's husband. Someone's father. He could have very well been my own.

He was once a voice that now has been silenced forever.

Suddenly, I smell blood and all the strength leaves my legs.

I drop to my knees on the filthy stone church floor. It hurts, but my feelings of dread and anguish are much more intense. So I stay there for a bit, attempting to pull myself together.

All the while, the song continues to play and, for the second time in my life, I associate music with something terrifying.

The first time was when I froze up on the stage, the day that could have brought us our much-desired success. We were all there. The whole band, ready to perform. But I put everything on the line.

I remember feeling a drop of cold sweat trickle down my back. I remember my heart thumping like it could pop out of my chest. I remember my hands trembling. Then, I ran to the bathroom and vomited so much that I thought my throat would rip open. I couldn't breathe and I was sure I was going to die. Then everything went dark.

Those same feelings take hold of me, but somehow, I manage to keep myself together.

A lump in my throat hardens, which rises up in the form of violent vomit.

Every pint of beer comes up all at once.

Which makes me feel slightly better, at least physically.

I wipe my mouth with the back of my hand, take a deep breath and stand up.

What should I do?

If I stay here, the police arrive and may even consider me a suspect.

But I need to know more. I need to understand all the coincidences that link the Psycho Killer to me.

My train of thought is interrupted by the sound of footsteps outside. They're here.

I find a broken window and escape through it. I flee the crime scene and run home.

I didn't sleep a wink.

Even as exhausted as I am, I can't get the scene out of my head. The body, the blood, the music.

And the place.

Why, out of all the dark corners of this district, did the killer have to choose that exact church?

I've viewed and reviewed the whole string of events, memories and details in my mind a million times over, but I come out empty-handed.

Frustrated, I realise that my efforts are in vain and I decide it's time to think about something else.

Soon it will be time for yet another day at work and I'm, quite literally, broken. I'd better take a shower and get ready.

On the way to the bathroom, I'm startled by the sound of a vibration.

My phone.

It's an unknown number.

Does someone know where I've been? Could the killer have found me?

With my heart racing, I press my phone against my ear.

"Hello?"

"Good morning, is this David?" asks a female voice on the other end of the line.

"Yes, it's me, who's calling?"

"Sorry for calling so early in the morning. This is Susan Shawn, I'm a detective with the London police."

No way.

The police have found me. I must have left behind a clue of some sort at the crime scene and now I'm a suspect. If they found out my connection to that church, then they must be absolutely certain that I'm involved.

"You called us recently, didn't you?", continues the detective.

"Yes... Yes..."

That's right. I'd left all my contact information when I called Scotland Yard. Maybe I'm in the clear.

"Well, it seems like you were right that the Psycho Killer would strike again", she continues, "and you were right about the song that would be playing at the crime scene."

I don't say anything in response, but the detective quickly breaks the silence again:

"I want to talk with you right now. Come to King's Cross station in 20 minutes. I'll be waiting."

She hangs up without giving me the chance to say anything.

Looks like work will have to wait.

I take a quick shower and arrive at the meeting place early.

While I wait, I think about what I'm doing.

Why am I putting myself in the middle of something so complicated and dangerous? My life was just starting to sort itself out...

But sorted out doesn't mean good, David, I tell myself automatically.

Even though my response sounds straight out of a self-help book, I can't deny the truth it holds.

I could get healthier, have better habits, and have a steady job. But if this is the right path, why do I constantly feel empty?

Why is there a hole in my chest?

I don't know. All I know is that this whole Psycho Killer story has made me feel more alive than I have in a long time. I need to know more. I need to figure out what's happening to me.

My thoughts are interrupted by the sounds of high heels clicking against the floor. I lift my eyes and see a woman, around 40 years old, a beautiful one at that.

I think it's strange to notice her beauty, given the circumstances, but it's impossible to ignore. She's a stunning mix of Whitney Houston in her prime and Angela Bassett in the 90s.

She spots me and walks towards me.

I can feel her powerful presence from afar. That can only be Detective Susan Shawn.

"You must be David", she says, stopping in front of me.

"Yes, nice to meet you."

"Nice to meet you, too, I'm Susan. I'm going to order myself some coffee in that coffee shop over there. In the meantime, you're going to tell me how you found out which song would be playing during the murder."

By the tone of her elegant, but extremely firm voice, I understand that this is not an invitation.

We sit across from each other at a table at the back of Caffè Nero. Susan orders a black coffee, no sugar. I order the same.

While we get our dose of caffeine, she explains to me how the police received a phone call from a homeless man who usually sleeps in the church. That's how they found out about the body and the song.

I try to act normal, but I feel my body tense up. And what if the homeless man saw me? And what if Susan invited me here to arrest me?

In an attempt to hide my discomfort, I take a sip of my coffee.

"But that's not what I called you here today", says Susan. "It doesn't matter how we discover crimes. I want to know how you put together the details."

"I just made the connection between the most successful songs that happened on the day of each crime and–"

"But why the year 1988?" she interrupts.

I take another sip before answering.

"It's the year I was born… my father had a CD of that year's greatest hits."

"I see." "And you found this correlation on the internet?"

"Not exactly," I respond. "The web helps, but it's not exactly reliable. I used my memories. I've always had a bit of a…different memory."

This time, it's her turn to take a sip from her cup.

As she drinks, she carefully analyses me.

She knows that I'm keeping secrets. It's better to get it out on the table.

"But that's not the only thing I discovered," I continue.

The closer she leans toward me, the harder it becomes to breathe.

"I think that I not only am able to discover the song that is going to play at the crime scenes but also where they will take place."

"Come again?", she says, surprised. "Why didn't you call us about this information?"

"When I called, I realised that what I had to say wasn't as important as I thought. After all, you're trained investigators, with databases and have access to the internet…"

"As you said so yourself, that's not a very reliable source."

She leans back in her chair, sitting in a more relaxed posture.

"Did you know that the crime would happen around here?"

I nod my head.

"Do you know when the next crime will happen?"

"Not exactly, but…"

"But you're capable of finding out", she says to finish my sentence.

"I think so," I reply.

Susan gets up in one swift movement, pulling on her coat that was hanging on the chair beside her.

"Great," she says. "Then let's work together."

Future

"I'm not used to throwing concerts in churches," says the young man standing before the audience. "But I hope that our Father in Heaven blesses me with this version…anyone here a fan of Belinda Carlisle?"

Several hands reach for the singer and he calls one of them up to the stage.

The guitar plays the first chords of *Heaven Is a Place on Earth*, by Belinda Carlisle, and then the performer and the fan start singing together.

The show is the first one ever to be held in the Saint Pancras Church, located next to King's Cross Underground station, one of the busiest in the city of London.

Side A

Track 4

"When the night falls down

I wait for you, and you come around

And the world's alive

With the sound of kids on the street outside..."

Heaven Is A Place On Earth - Belinda Carlisle

Past

"Good morning, sleepy head", said the father, softly stroking his hair until he woke. "You went to bed already dressed for today, did you?"

"Of course. It's for luck in today's game! We're going to need it!"

The duo, who went to bed wearing their favourite team's red shirt, got in the car ready to face four hours on the road, from the heart of London to Liverpool.

The destination? The legendary Anfield stadium, where the home team will face off against their rival, Everton.

Now playing: *Desire* by U2.

Present

Susan drops me off at home leaving me with the mission of aiding the investigation with my musical repertoire.

From the looks of it, I'm not considered a suspect nor did I leave any clues at this morning's scene. Still, I can't remain completely calm.

I have a strong feeling that these crimes have something to do with me and, as much as my rational side says that this is impossible, I can't cast the idea away.

Every musician is a bit egocentric. I don't want to fall back into my old superhero syndrome, but the first three songs the Psycho Killer chose, follow the exact same order as my dad's CD…and if my memory serves me right, the next one will be even more important to me.

This idea echoed in the back of my mind ever since I set foot in that macabre church, but I think part of me didn't want to believe it.

I do a quick internet search in hopes of being wrong, but deep down I know that won't be the case.

After excluding sites and blogs of questionable accuracy, I find the proof I'm looking for.

On June 4th, 1998, the number one song on the radio was *Heaven Is a Place On Earth* by Belinda Carlisle.

The first song I sang in my choir.

I take a deep breath and throw my laptop to the side. I stand up and pace around the room, trying to come up with a plausible explanation for this madness.

Looks like everything is connected to my past, but who could possibly know about it?

The first person that comes to mind is my old man. But I don't want to feed into the hope that he's still alive.

And, if he were, he'd never be responsible for something like this.

I avoid thinking about him because the memories are much too painful, but this time I can't escape them.

I often say that I left The Sunflowers for emotional reasons, which technically isn't a lie, but in reality, it is much deeper than that.

When I was 17, our band was a local phenomenon. We formed a trio with me, on vocals and lead guitar, James Edgard, on the bass, and Alex Crawford, on drums.

My father eventually took on the business side of things.

Although we'd never been featured on the radio or abroad, we were very well-known in the alternative scene in London and filled up pubs every weekend with our shows.

Until one day, we had a shot at achieving one of my biggest dreams: performing in Glastonbury, the largest rock event in England.

Our debut would have been just one month after our invitation. Generally, artists are invited with more of a heads-up, but due to a cancellation, we were called at the last minute.

We would play our alternative music on the stage that introduced The Killers, Franz Ferdinand and other legends to the world.

Obviously, we rehearsed like crazy, practising unedited tracks and incredible covers. When the big day arrived, we were more than ready.

At least that's what I thought.

My dad drove us there like he always did: in his 1977 Mustang. My old man was very charming and his car was part of the show, especially since he had the incredible habit of dressing and acting like he was still living in the 70s.

It wasn't uncommon to see him wearing chequered shirts, bell bottoms and leather boots. And that's exactly what he was wearing to take us to the night of our lives.

In his car, which was impeccably preserved, except for the radio, which was upgraded to a more modern model that could play CDs. And on that day, the usual CD was playing, Hot 88.

My dad must have noticed that we were anxious, but he had a knack for always knowing how to calm our nerves. That's why he told us stories the whole way from London to Glastonbury about the times he'd been there and the shows he'd seen, including his first one in 1970.

At the time, the event was still called the "Pilton Pop, Folk & Blues Festival". The main attraction was The Kinks, which would close its doors on Saturday, September 19. Both of these events were enough to sell out Worthy Farm entirely, which is where the magic happened. But the day before the fateful day, an unfortunate event was the catalyst for an unforgettable opening act: Jimmy Hendrix's passing.

The death of a legend inspired every group to come together and throw an unforgettable tribute.

I remember that, as he was telling his story, my old man started tearing up and we, who up until that moment were feeling extremely tense, had completely forgotten why we had felt that way.

Arriving at our destination, the staff greeted us with kindness and directed us to our dressing room. We didn't let our reception get to our heads, but the food and comfort we received gave us the unprecedented feeling that we really were important.

We played some tunes, I sang like never before and left for my pre-show routine, feeling confident that we were just minutes away from making history.

Before warming up my voice, I stretched and practiced some power posing, to both calm me down and hype me up at the same time. I went through my usual routine, but while getting into my first pose, something strange happened.

I felt like my heart was about to pop out of my chest.

It was beating so fast that it felt like it could stop at any moment. Additionally, I started to imagine the worst possible scenarios: me going up on stage and being booed, forgetting the lyrics, people leaving before the end of the song...

Today, I understand what was happening. I had a panic attack, something I had never experienced before.

But at the time, I thought that I was about to die.

I called for my father, who came running, white as a ghost.

"Dad, I can't do it", I gasped.

"What do you mean?"

"I'm dying."

"Dying?"

He checked over my body, expecting to find an injury or something physically wrong with me, but of course, nothing was wrong.

"My heart's racing, it feels like it's going to explode."

"Calm down", he said soothingly. "Lay here in my lap."

"I can't."

"Son, you're nervous, this is natural."

"No, Dad, you don't understand", I yelled as my nervousness continued to consume me. "I'm sorry." Tell the band that the show's over.

Hearing me like this, he hugged me tightly and said:

"Son, the choice is yours." "I love you regardless if you get up on that stage or not." "But I assure you, you're not dying, what you're feeling is very normal and..."

I don't let him finish.

I ran away and disappeared into the night.

Ah, if only I'd known that those would be the last words I'd hear from him.

After that, I don't know what happened. I only know the stories people have told me:

My dad told the guys about my decision. They even tried to go on stage without me, since James Edgard had a good voice and knew all the words to our songs, but it wasn't enough to save the show. Since I was the face of the band, the producers preferred to cancel the performance.

I don't remember ever seeing James or Alex after my episode.

The rehearsal for the performance that never happened was the last time I went up on stage.

And the words that I exchanged with my dad were the last, before his passing. Which happened that very night.

The Mustang that we loved so much was found at the bottom of the Thames River, near the London Eye. The expert identified that the car had clear break malfunctions and was the probable cause of the accident. A steep price to pay for driving a relic with hard-to-replace parts.

The body was never found, but after years of searching, the police declared my father dead.

We held a funeral without a casket, instead we gathered around his photos.

"When I feel alone

I reach for you and you bring me home

When I'm lost at sea

I hear your voice and it carries me"

Belinda Carlisle - Heaven Is A Place On Earth

My life ended that night. My biggest hero was gone. And with it, so was my dream of changing the world through music.

Thinking about it ties my stomach into knots, not only for reliving one of the most painful moments in my life but also for associating my father with the damn Psycho Killer.

No. My old man would never be involved in this.

Who else could know all of these details about me? Who else would even know the songs that I sang as a child? This can't be just a coincidence.

I sit back down on the couch, my mind racing despite such a hectic night.

I return to my memories in the choir and the people who sang with me at the time. After all, my relationship with the other songs could just be a coincidence, but to have a murder held in the place where I learned how to sing can't be the work of chance.

Racking my brain for my fellow choristers, I recall an old photo that I posted on Facebook of me and the group, class of 1995.

I pull out my phone from my pocket, open the app, and after a few minutes find what I was looking for.

In the photo, I see myself, James and Alex, my band members, the teacher, Charles Boyce, and various other boys whose names I can't remember.

The same band members I haven't contacted since my panic attack. My choir teacher was an active part of the first years of my life, but afterwards, I never saw him again.

I refuse to believe that one of them would be a suspect, but I need to know every detail about our rehearsals, who was there, and if there was any abnormal behaviour. They are the best shot I have for unravelling this mystery.

Finding James and Alex on social media is easy. I start to get cold feet before sending a message and I know very well that, after having snuffed out their dreams in Glastonbury, they may not give me the time of day…

But with lives on the line, I can't afford to not try.

I gather my courage and send a confident message suggesting a one-on-one meeting with each one.

Now all I can do is wait.

I glance at the clock.

I should already be at work, but who could clean records at a time when their hands are full with a real murder mystery? A case that, on top of everything, involves music and my own past?

I'm standing at a crossroad of a moral dilemma.

Stability vs possibility.

My job at Rough Trade pays the bills.

But the mystery that haunts London's streets gives my life meaning.

Between certainty and doubt, I go with the latter.

Forgive me, life duties, but I need to understand what's happening and the next step is to discover the scene of this night's crime.

I'm certain that the music that will be playing at the next homicide will be *Heaven is a Place on Earth* by Belinda Carlisle, but what matters most is where it will happen.

Where did Belinda first sing this song?

I feel my heart pounding, just as it did in Glastonbury, which makes it harder to gather my thoughts.

Everything mixes together like a sound, place, and date salad, and I start to worry that I might have another anxiety attack.

Ever since the first time this happened, near the stage that could have changed my life, I was never able to handle situations like these very well.

I try taking some deep breaths and even try meditating, but nothing helps.

You can't back out now, David, I think to myself. *Susan trusts you.*

The guys from our band trusted me too.

I let them down.

That's it.

I tell myself.

If you aren't going to help catch this Psycho Killer, you'll never get the chance to do something noteworthy again. After missing out on the huge shot that you had in the past, are you going to make the same mistake again?

If my new habits don't help calm me down, perhaps my old ones will do the trick.

I light a cigarette and pour myself a shot of whisky.

I pick up my guitar and sing a few of Belinda Carlisle's songs.

In the time that it takes for me to empty my first glass, I feel my thoughts start to organise themselves.

I don't come to a solution, but my memories give me a few good places to start.

I play a little more. Smoke a little more. Drink a little more.

But the final answer that I'm looking for never comes to me.

I can't call Susan with possibilities. I need a definite answer. One that can only come from me.

After an insistent half-hour of trying, I give in to the idea that my head is too much of a mess and that my memories alone won't come up with an answer. So I resort to something I have no other choice to use.

I go to Google for help once again.

I don't fully trust it, but at least Google isn't drunk and sleep-deprived.

I check dates, double-check my facts, until I find the answer.

Belinda Carlisle performed *Heaven Is A Place On Earth* for the world in a pocket show on a small boat in the tunnels of the Islington canal.

I call Detective Shaw to reveal what I've discovered.

> "So what you're saying is that the next death…" she says.

> "Will be in some abandoned land close to the Islington tunnels" I confirm.

Silence rings out after my declaration, but I'm able to make out my partner's breathing over the phone. She must be thinking about something.

> "Look," I say, breaking the silence, "I'm certain that you'll be able to catch this bastard and I wish you all the luck in the world…"

> "You wish us all the luck in the world", she interrupts.

> "Come again?"

I switch my phone to the other ear, confused about what I just heard.

> "You're wishing us luck", she repeats, "You're coming with me."

And that's how became officially involved in the investigation of the crime that's shocking England.

I hang up the call feeling partly nervous, partly elated.

I'm important. I can make a difference with my musical knowledge.

A second chance, after throwing my first one in the trash.

Even standing before a happy realisation, an indescribable fatigue washes over me and all I want to do is sleep.

But I need to find my motorbike, which I left near the chapel, and I also need to explain this to my work somehow.

But my eyes are so heavy.

I think I'm just going to rest them for a little bit…

"When the night falls down

I wait for you

And you come around…"

Heaven Is A Place On Earth - Belinda Carlisle

I wake up with the setting sun.

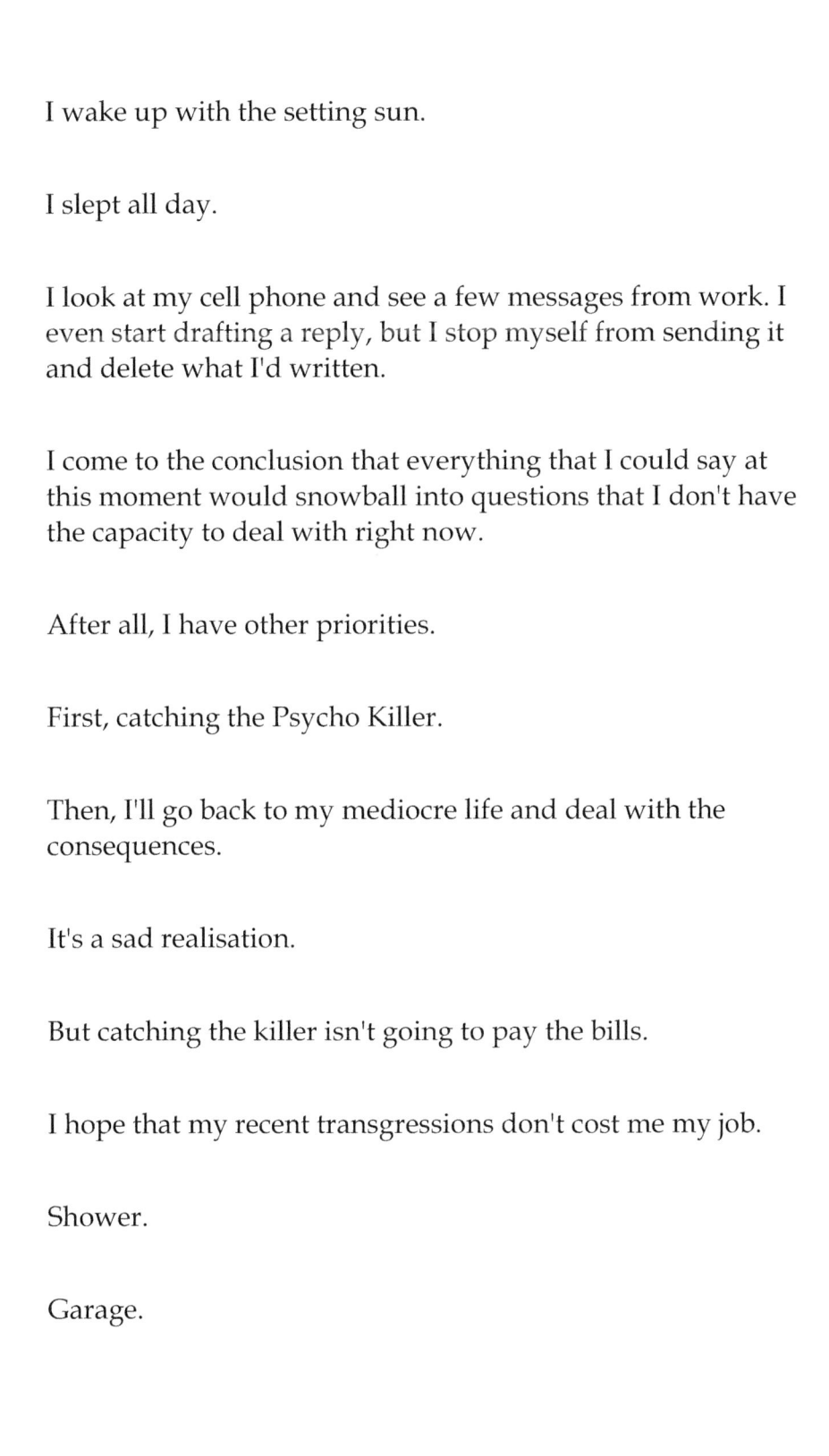

I slept all day.

I look at my cell phone and see a few messages from work. I even start drafting a reply, but I stop myself from sending it and delete what I'd written.

I come to the conclusion that everything that I could say at this moment would snowball into questions that I don't have the capacity to deal with right now.

After all, I have other priorities.

First, catching the Psycho Killer.

Then, I'll go back to my mediocre life and deal with the consequences.

It's a sad realisation.

But catching the killer isn't going to pay the bills.

I hope that my recent transgressions don't cost me my job.

Shower.

Garage.

Motorbike.

I stop by a local pub to eat and to prepare myself for the big event that I'll witness in a few hours.

This morning, we'll protect someone's father.

We'll bring a villain to justice.

We'll save lives through music.

I'll be part of it.

Who knows, in the spotlight of our success, may finally be able to come to terms with my father's death.

My irresponsibility cost him his life in the past.

May my current courage compensate for my flawed past self.

And may the acceptance of all these feelings allow me to play once again.

Maybe my job at Rough Trade wouldn't be the reason I keep my lights on.

But in order for this to happen, I need to give my best today.

Carried by my hopes, I wait until 3 in the morning.

My alarm goes off on the dot.

I'm at the meeting point on Florence Street, waiting for Susan.

This residential area is so beautiful that it doesn't deserve to have a crime happen nearby.

From there, we head for the Islington canals.

Dare I feel optimistic that we've arrived at the scene before the killer, but Susan quickly cuts me down a size.

> "Of course, it's important to find out where the crimes will happen, but think, David. The most important thing is to understand the Psycho Killer's criteria for choosing his victims. We already know that they are men around the age of 60. Still, that's very little to go on."

She's absolutely right.

Aside from my personal attempt to reconnect with the King's Cross choir members, I need to figure out the connection between the Psycho Killer and his victims.

Thinking about it now, I realise that I was so involved with the possibility of catching the killer that I forgot to check my messages for the last few hours.

I open up Instagram, and to my surprise, I'm greeted with unread messages from James, my childhood friend and the bass player from my former band:

"Hey David! It's been a while! I'd love to meet up. I'm a music teacher at the London Music Academy in Clapham Town. How about we grab a coffee after work?"

I'm surprised but above all happy with the message.

Although I'd only seen the message now, he replied to me minutes after I'd reached out to him. So I think that James isn't holding a grudge about what happened at Glastonbury.

The talented bass player was one of my closest childhood friends and the opportunity to connect with him, in a music school of all places, brings back great memories. I wonder if scheduling a meet-up with him tomorrow is the best use of my time since we have no idea what will happen in the next few hours, but since I'm fresh out of ideas, I agree to his plans.

My childhood memories are soon diluted by the sudden realisation of what time it is.

It's already almost 4, and if the crime is going to happen here, it'll be any minute now.

Susan leads me to a dark space, similar to the areas the killer had chosen before.

We're in a shed where the owners store their nautical equipment.

My first impression of the location makes me completely forget about London's organisation and cleanliness. The claustrophobic space strongly resembles a horror movie: a room full of cobwebs and rusty devices.

It has to be here, I think.

Suddenly, I feel the hairs stand up on the back of my neck. I don't know if my body's ever been so alert in my life.

To relieve the tension, I try to rationalise the situation.

Easy, David. The whole area is surrounded by the police. We're going to be alright.

That's when I hear a barely audible whisper in my ear.

"What's your favourite band?"

It's Susan.

She's so close to me that I can smell the mint in her breath.

"My what?" I say louder than I'd have liked. "But why do you…"

She puts her finger to my lips, clearly asking me to be quiet. Then the conversation continues in a whisper:

> "Since we're here, alone, waiting…why not break a bit of the tension?"

My tension, that is, after all, my partner is extremely relaxed for someone in such a grim situation.

Ok, I'll bite.

> "This question is almost impossible for me to answer. But I can give you 4: Queen, U2, Bob Dylan and Bruce Springsteen. It's an even split between bands from the UK and solo artists from the United States. What do you think?"
>
> "I see", says Susan, "You're one of those who only likes old stuff."
>
> "Definitely not!" I reply, again, at a volume louder than is appropriate for someone who's at a probable crime scene.

Susan gives me a look as if she were scolding a clueless teenager, and I raise my hands in a silent apology.

She comes closer to me again and whispers.

> "Then tell me about some newer bands and artists, because so far I'm already very familiar with the bands you've mentioned."

I'm not going to lie. She has surprised me. In a good way.

I answer:

"So how about Coldplay, The Killers, John Mayer and Ben Howard?"

"Do you always give two from the US and two from the UK?"

"Ah, no. Total coincidence."

"And the fact that they're all overplayed, is that also a coincidence?"

Now she's rubbing salt in the wound.

"What do you mean, overplayed?"

"I also like these ones that you've mentioned, but I think you still aren't getting my question. Please tell me about a band I haven't heard of."

If she's doing this to ease my nerves, it's working.

Soon after, my mind travels through the musical world and almost forgets about the horrors that could happen around us.

I choose two bands that I think she's never heard of and say:

"The Gaslight Anthem and 1975".

"That's it," she says. "I have no idea who you're talking about…"

"To me, The Gaslight Anthem is the best rock band since the Foo Fighters," I explain. "Imagine if Bruce Springsteen had played with The Ramones. It's like that."

Susan raises her eyebrows, wearing a mixed expression of surprise and satisfaction. I think she liked my suggestion.

"And what's the best track on their best album?" she asks, her phone in her hands, ready to take notes.

That's when it rings, nearly giving both of us a heart attack.

The light expression from Susan's face changes immediately. She knits her brow and opens her messaging app.

Her expression grows more grim the more she reads whatever's written there. Then she lifts her eyes to meet mine.

"What?", I ask.

"He's done it, David."

I put my hands on my head.

"What do you mean, he's done it? Where?"

I scour our surroundings with my eyes, trying to find anything that slightly resembles a killer.

> "It wasn't here", Susan explains.

It wasn't here? That's not possible? It has to be here!

I'm lost. Shocked.

> "It was near Grosvenor Gardens, in a vacant lot", Susan continues. "With the usual beheading and vinyl covered in blood playing *Heaven is a Place On Earth.*"
>
> "No," I reply, when it finally hits me. "No, no, no, no…"

I pace aimlessly back and forth. Susan follows me with her eyes.

> "How could I have been so stupid?", I say.
>
> "What happened, David?"
>
> "The crime was close to Victoria Station?"
>
> "Exactly", said Susan.

I feel my legs start to weaken, so I sit down.

I can't believe that another person's dead…and this time it's my fault. Because of my idiocy. My irresponsibility cost another life. As if my father's hadn't been enough.

"David, what happened?," says Susan, kneeling down beside me.

"What makes this song different from all the other ones found at the crime scene?"

"I don't know."

"It wasn't composed by the performer herself."

I cover my face in my hands as if I could hide my shame in them.

"*Save Me, Belfast Son* and *Killer* are all songs written by the performers themselves. While *Heaven Is A Place On Earth* wasn't composed by Belinda Carlisle."

"Who did then?"

"I have no idea, but I'm willing to bet that the real composer performed the song for the first time somewhere close to Belgrave Square Garden."

I hear Susan relay all the information I've just told her to her team.

Idiot. I'm such an idiot.

My stomach churns and my head starts spinning.

"Susan…", I call over in a whisper.

A bitterness rises into my mouth.

"Susan", I call again, this time louder.

My heartbeat accelerates to a violent pace. I feel like I'm going to die.

"SUSAN", I yell, before passing out.

"In this world, we're just beginnin'

To understand the miracle of livin'

Baby, I was afraid before

But I'm not afraid anymore…"

Heaven Is A Place On Earth - Belinda Carslile

The light from the sun's first rays creeping through my window wakes me up.

I'm in my apartment, lying in bed, after the shameful event that happened this morning.

In addition to failing Susan, disrupting the investigation, and being musically humiliated by the Psycho Killer, I somehow managed to pass out.

What a model rock star.

I feel like a huge failure.

I preferred living with the fact that I'm not doing what I love.

But at least in the record shop, there were no risks.

When I take on something bigger, what happens?

People die.

The passing of the man who brought me into this world wasn't enough to teach my huge ego this hard lesson.

And now there's another coffin because of me.

Susan warned me about this feeling.

She told me that when you try to save a life and fail, you feel responsible for that death. She said that I need to be careful to not be swallowed up by that darkness.

In a way, I already knew about this.

Ever since Glastonbury.

I just swept the feeling under the rug.

And it seems like this is exactly what I'm going through.

Now? In the face of recidivism?

The feeling hits hard.

My thoughts spiral into destructive ones, only being interrupted by a fitful and restless sleep.

I miss work, again.

I refuse to get out of bed.

Gathered under my front door, I spot scattered bills starting to accumulate.

How the hell am I going to pay for all of this if I get fired?

A ping from my phone snaps me back to reality.

It's James, he sent me a picture of us rehearsing together over 10 years ago on WhatsApp. Captioned with the affectionate message:

"Excited to see you soon."

The horrors I faced early this morning made me forget about the meet-up with my childhood friend.

I get out of bed, determined not to miss it. But first, I still have a few hours to minimise the damage I've done.

I brew a strong coffee - no alcohol this time - and focus on meditating. Then, I put aside everything that I have that can be useful against the Psycho Killer: songs, newspapers, encyclopaedias, newspaper clippings, and of course, my memories.

A few hours of focused work allows me to draw a timeline of likely songs and crime scenes for the next two occurrences.

For Psycho Killer's next attack, the music will be *Desire* by U2. The single was first performed at the Jubilee Gardens, near the London Eye.

Then, it'll be *Sacrifice* by Elton John. How suggestive.

I send all this to Susan, practically imploring her to double, triple and quadruple check if my information is correct.

And I leave to have a chat with my friend.

As I get ready, I remember the times we used to play together and I have a sudden urge to listen to our songs.

I take my headphones and put on *Starts With Pain*, it's my favourite out of all the songs we've written.

The music brings me the peace I so desperately need at this moment and gives me the confidence to believe that I can really do this. That not all is lost.

On my motorbike, I head to where my childhood friend is waiting for me. Out of the corner of my eye, I spot the cafe at the music school where he works.

I recognise James' smile from afar, but the rest of him has changed so much.

Instead of wearing his usual grunge band shirts like a good Nirvana and Pearl Jam fan, now he wears a typical teacher's outfit, a light sweater with a buttoned-up shirt underneath. His full, flowing hair is now a gleaming bald spot. It's strange. One of the biggest rock fans I've ever met, who tried his entire life to look like Kurt Cobain and Eddie Vedder, now looks more like Moby[1].

"David", he calls out, "Over here."

"James, it's been so long."

"It really has been, we haven't seen each other since…"

He stops himself, understanding that talking about my crisis may not be something I'm ready to talk about yet.

He pulls me into a bro hug as a means of diverting from his unfinished sentence and we sit down at one of the coffee tables.

"So, what's it like to teach music?" I ask to steer the conversation further away from my past.

---

[1] An electronic music star, totally bald.

> "Oh man, it's fantastic. There are so many talented kids and teens that go here. It reminds me of us, full of dreams and energy."

And with that, we take a stroll through memory lane. When I feel like the mood is right and there's enough of a gap in our conversation, I ease the conversation into what I came here to talk about:

> "Speaking about our childhood, I wanted to talk to you about the choir, James."

> "You want to get back into singing?", he asks excitedly. "Man, I can help you with–"

> "It's not that", I interrupt gently. "It's that…well, you must be following the news about this Psycho Killer guy, right?"

He leans back a bit in his seat, looking me up and down suspiciously.

> "I don't usually read the newspaper, but of course I've heard of the story."

> "Yeah." "What I'm about to ask you might sound a bit strange, but do you think that somebody from our old choir group could have done this?"

Almost immediately, James' eyebrows pull together, leaving creases on his forehead.

> "What do you mean? What gave you that idea?"

"It's a long story," I say, "but to sum it up, the impression I have is that the killer knows me somehow. All the songs that were played at the scene of the crime have some sort of connection to me."

Then James relaxes, shakes his head and flashes a smile.

"And what song in the history of music doesn't, David?" he asks.

"What do you mean?"

"Man, we're addicted to music. Take some obscure song, for example, I guarantee that we'll find ourselves connected to it somehow."

I think he senses my confusion, so he leans towards me and continues his explanation:

"I've already fallen into this trap before. Every time a girl told me about her favourite band I thought 'Wow, she's my soulmate'. It was only after 10 girls in a row who eventually showed their true colours that I realised that I'm the one who likes all these groups and that the girls weren't perfect matches for me."

Is this the answer to the question that burns so intensely inside me?

The relationship between the songs' release locations and the murder scenes has been proven, but maybe the personal involvement I'm dead set on seeing really is just an ego trap.

I let James take the lead in our conversation. We end up talking a bit more about the good old times, which distracts me from bloodied disks and decapitated corpses.

"Remember when we skipped mass to watch United vs City?"

How could I not?

We snuck out during the Holy Communion and slipped into the nearest pub. At the peak of the second-half, Alex's extremely religious mum found us. Drinking beer, no less.

We were forced to spend two hours kneeling and asking the heavens for forgiveness.

Good times.

Aside from music, James, Alex and I also shared a passion for football. Although I'm from London, I'm a Red. James is a Blue and Alex is a Gunner. Our favourite teams always provided us with lots of moments with laughter, jests and rivalries.

But when we went out on the field together, we understood each other perfectly.

The three of us were the backbone of our own team that we called "the King's Cross United". James was a very serious defender and an excellent shot, with controlled passes, but was never afraid to go on the attack when the game asked him to. I was more of the classic midfielder, who preferred making assists over scoring goals. And Alex, he was the centre forward sent from the heavens. There were countless games where James would get the ball, pass it to me and I'd kick it to Alex who'd secure the goal. We even had a secret, pre-choreographed victory dance.

We had so many great memories together but, now that we're talking about this, one of the not-so-positive ones begs for the spotlight.

It was a Saturday. We'd played and won against a neighbourhood team. As usual, we went to celebrate our success at James' house with our promised Shepherd's Pie waiting for us.

That was the tradition. Losing calories on the field only to gain them all back by eating as much as possible while watching sports on TV.

The Chelsea vs Tottenham, a classic London rivalry. I remember this moment not just because of the incredible game, but mainly because on this specific day, James' dad, Cedrick, was watching the game with us.

He was a Chelsea fanatic and often broke cups, plates and even armchairs in front of us. Only on this day, it was even worse. The *Blues* were losing, but James didn't seem to pay any mind. In fact, he was paying so little attention to the scoreboard that he started humming one of our songs while the game was on.

> "I already told you to stop with that gay shit, especially on game day," said Cedrick, "don't you see it's bad luck?"

James didn't mean any harm. He was on another planet, like he always was, completely focused on the song.

> "Hey, are you listening to me, boy? Shut up!"

To make things worse, Tottenham scores...again.

And then his words became action.

He stood up abruptly and dragged my friend by his hair to his bedroom. We could only imagine what was happening from the furious screams, cries of pain, and violent noises.

We didn't know what to do, until Cedrick's wife asked us to leave.

After that, our friend didn't show up for choir or football practice for a week, probably recovering from the abuse.

The bitter memory brings me back to reality.

Maybe I'm reading too much into this whole Psycho Killer incident. Maybe it really has nothing to do with me.

But this doesn't mean that I can't help.

After all, he's still out there and will try to kill again.

I can help stop the criminal. If not for me, to honour my father.

And find meaning in the night that has ruined my life to this day.

More than discovering songs or places, what really will make the difference is discovering who will be the next victim.

I still have a few hours until the Psycho Killer strikes again, so I decide to wrap up our meeting.

>"It was nice seeing you, James."

>"It really was, Dave. Let's do this more often."

I get on my motorbike and return home.

When I get there, I'm amazed to see that I have another unread message on my phone. This time from the guy that taught me everything I know about music.

Future

Anxiety attacks are things of the past, but today, the young man is nervous like never before.

Not for nothing, either, because he's about to play for more than 50,000 people at Anfield Stadium, Liverpool's home field, the team that he's been cheering for ever since he was a little boy.

He steps on stage wearing one of the team's official red jerseys, and the fans go wild.

> "Good evening, Anfield."

The crowd responds in unison.

> "I always dreamed of being here. As a kid, on the field, and now, on stage. To mark this special occasion, I'll start with something new. A song that I know you all love, but also holds a special place in my heart."

Starting my concerts with a cover is pretty standard, but this time, for the first time, he'll be performing a medley of covers.

He sings only the first few verses of *You'll Never Walk Alone*, the home team's anthem, without any instruments accompanying his voice.

The crowd sings along. The chorus is deafening.

While the crowd continues to sing the first song, the young man starts playing the beggining chords of *Desire* by U2.

Side B

Track 5

"She's the candle

Burning in my room

I'm like the needle

Needle and spoon

Over the counter

With a shotgun

Pretty soon everybody's got one"

Desire - U2

Past

"Ah, in that case you could really only be over here…", said the father, after finally finding the boy.

When he woke up, he went to his son's room only to find it empty. At first, he had the usual parental panic and turned the house upside down, calling out for him desperately. But then, after rationalising his thoughts, he made an educated guess on where he would be.

He went to the garage and there he was, in the car with a CD in his hands.

It was *Sleeping With The Past* by Elton John. The chosen soundtrack for our journey to Oxford.

The reason for our trip? Music.

It wasn't uncommon for the father and son to choose a destination for no reason in particular, but rather for the pretext of driving somewhere with the windows down, wind hitting their faces, all while listening to their favourite songs.
PAREI AQUI

Present

"Meet me the day after tomorrow, at 1 in the afternoon at the Borough Market."

This is all that was written in Mr. Boyce's message.

Straight to the point as ever, I think.

Our meeting is right in the middle of working hours. But what's one more day to someone who's already on an irresponsible streak?

I respond, confirming my attendance and, soon after, I send a message to Susan, asking if she's checked over the information I sent. If this time I'm able to help.

She doesn't reply back.

Instead, she calls me, which makes me jump out of my skin.

"Hi", I say.

"Hi."

Then, a strange silence fills the air.

Did I disappoint her that much?

> "So, did I manage to be useful this time or have I dropped the ball again?" I ask to break the silence.

I remember the smell of blood when I came across one of the Psycho Killer's victims. I remember his slashed throat and the empty expression on his face.

> "Someone died because of the Psycho Killer," said Susan. "He's the one to blame. Just him."

I don't reply this time, so she keeps talking:

> "Actually, you've helped us streamline things a lot around here." "But it's not just that…"

I sit on the couch and switch the ear I'm holding my phone to, paying close attention to what she wants to tell me.

> "You know, David, I noticed that there's something more to your story. There's something there between you and the killer," she seems to be searching for the right words before continuing. "My instinct tells me that you and he share a connection, similar tastes…"

Does she consider me a suspect now?

Am I a suspect?

I might be going crazy and that would explain a lot…

It would explain my connection to the songs. My connection to the chapel. My feeling of unease.

I haven't been sleeping well and, if I'm being honest with myself, I hate to admit it but something inside of me hasn't been right for a long time now.

Insanity?

Split personality?

Sleepwalking?

Accomplices?

It's better for me to talk than for her to find out.

    "Susan…" I interrupt her, "I need to tell you something about me."

Then I tell her everything.

I reveal my connection with the songs, from *Save Me* to *Desire*. My past at the King's Cross church, and how I tested my vocal limits in my choir. About how the first song I ever sang was *Heaven Is A Place On Earth*. I tell her about the CD "Hot '88" that my dad always played in the car. I also talk about what happened at Glastonbury and finish with the cases of "murders" in my personal life: I got back into playing, smoking, singing, drinking, driving my motorbike and dressing like a rockstar.

> "Something's definitely not right."

> "I agree with you", I conclude.

Again, silence.

The only sound being the one of my heart, almost ripping open my chest.

I'm not used to sharing things about myself, but at the heart of my fear and shame, I feel a certain comfort.

Now she knows and, whatever is about to happen isn't in my hands.

> "Thanks for sharing all this with me", she says. "There really is something off about all this. That's the nature of my work. Of the universe that we've ended up in."

She realises that I'm not really following her and tries to expand on her explanation.

> "I've trained for this job, I'm really good at what I do. Even then, after dealing with the worst crimes, I still get shaken up. I often doubt myself. That's what it takes to take evil head-on…and you and this evil that we're chasing are connected."

She pauses, making sure that I'm following along. I am. I'm following every word.

> "Both you and the Psycho Killer see your calling in music. It's what drives both of you. But his motivation is corrupted. He wants to use music to kill and wreak havoc, while you want…"

> "To save lives through music," I finish her sentence.

As soon as I say these words out loud, I feel a little better. It's like magic.

> "Music isn't evil, David. And neither are you," says Susan. "Just the way the killer is making use of music is what makes it evil. And this is messing with your head."

> "I see."

> "And that's why I want your help," she adds. "These songs are as important to you as they are to him…just in a completely different way."

She wants my help? Despite everything I've done and told her, she still wants my cooperation? Is that right?

"The Psycho Killer is going to strike again this morning and I'm going to try to stop him," she says. "It would be great to have you on my side."

I'm in. Obviously I'm in.

Night falls and Susan comes to pick me up. She parks the car along the Thames River bank near the London Eye, close to where my father's car was found.

Dad, if you're there, please lend me a hand, I ask silently.

Susan points out the way and we head to an abandoned car park near the Jubilee Gardens. According to police studies, this is the most plausible place for the crime to happen, following the Psycho Killer's patterns.

It's exactly 3:13 when we establish ourselves at the probable crime scene. Since the killer always strikes close to 4, we still have a bit of time to lay out our strategies.

Or not.

Susan's phone is once again the bearer of bad news.

"He's already done it", she says.

"What do you mean? It's too early."

"We didn't just get the time wrong, but also the place."

"Impossible. Where was the murder?"

"Nearby in the London Dungeons."

The London Dungeons. An abandoned tourist spot. Under maintenance.

Susan explains that the police even considered that spot, but thought it would be too obvious and risky, given the number of workers on site.

We rushed over to the spot and, in six minutes, we were facing a horror unlike any other.

"This crime doesn't follow the pattern", Susan immediately notices.

I look over everything carefully and soon understand what she means.

This time, the killer wasn't as careful. The vinyl is clearly scratched, the record player isn't in mint condition and even the body itself is in a different position than the other crimes…although it still makes my stomach churn and my blood pressure drops a little.

The only thing that's within the expectations is the music. *Desire* by U2 was playing when the police arrived on the scene.

"Something's seriously wrong here," says Susan. "But until we take a better look at the crime scene, I'm sorry to say that we're back to square one."

I stop for a moment to think and decide on a course of action.

I'm already up to my neck in this story, so why not see this out to the end?

"Actually, I don't think so," I say. "Maybe we do have a clue."

I explain to her that I met up with James, that I'm going to be meeting up with my old teacher and that I can still try to talk to Alex.

Like a woman on a mission, she suggests:

"If we leave now for Oxford, we can meet up with your friend and come back in time to have lunch with your tutor."

"So you don't think I'm crazy?"

"I don't know, but it's the only lead we have right now," she says. "The sooner we act the better, if we don't want to have another victim in our hands tomorrow morning."

"She's the dollars

She's my protection

She's a promise

In the year of election…"

Desire - U2

Alex still hasn't replied to me on Instagram, but thanks to social media, I discovered that he gives football lessons to children in Oxford and that the first class of the day is for kids under 13.

So that's where we're going.

My leather jacket will protect me from the wind. I hop on my motorbike, Triumph Bobber, with Susan riding pillion and I leave for Oxford with a smile on my face.

I know that making a trip like this on two wheels isn't the safest option, especially for someone who has been going non-stop and has barely slept, but I needed this.

The last few days have been tense like a thriller movie, but even in the face of all my fatigue and worries, it's impossible to not be enchanted by the sunrise.

It rises like an omen of a beautiful day. Maybe things will start to get better from here on out?

The last few days have been grey and long, but today seems like it might be a bit brighter. There's not a cloud in the sky and the temperature is getting warmer because of the approaching summer.

You may already be thinking this, but it's worth mentioning that I use headphones while I drive.

Don't do this at home. After all, ideally all your concentration should be on the road. Only the guy nicknamed DJ would always be listening to music and that's why, a playlist with all the songs I like the most from the Scottish band Biffy Clyro are packed along for the ride.

How did I convince Susan to let me do this? The answer's simple, I brought headphones for her too.

The first chords of *Biblical* echo in my ears and I feel a much-needed calmness wash over me. From my rear-view mirror, I can see that my partner is in tune with this feeling as well.

In addition to the scenic route from London to Oxford, the hit songs from one of my favourite rock bands and the spring sun, I imagine meeting up with Alex is going to be incredible.

I love the city and I love football, so having the chance to see him work in the business will be so interesting. On top of that, we'll be able to catch up on the good memories of our childhood.

When we arrive at our destination, I park my motorbike near Magdalen College.

It's 6:30 in the morning. There's still 30 minutes until my friend hits the fields. I'm going to make the most out of my time and visit a place that's very special to me and show it to my partner.

It's Fellows Garden, one of the most beautiful green spaces located at the heart of the institution.

I'll never forget the day that I came here for the first time in 2013. I was listening to random Bruce Springsteen songs and just as I was approaching the garden, *Secret Garden*, one of my favourite songs of his, started playing.

A shiver went up my spine and I felt the certainty that I was where I was supposed to be. The first chords of the beautiful melody made that moment sacred.

I entered through the gate, and continued following the path until I came across an unforgettable heart-shaped sculpture in the middle of a bush. The sight was metaphoric to me, because it was as if, at that moment, my own heart was exposed, just as I was exposed to the combination of music and nature.

Since then, *Secret Garden* has become my favourite track in the whole world.

I had liked the song ever since I heard it in the film *Jerry Maguire*[2], but after this work of fate, Bruce's ballad reached the top of my list.

I go through my tradition with Susan and hit play on the anthem as we enter the utopia.

My body shivers, as if I were experiencing the moment for the first time all over again.

We walk towards the sculpture and then sat down next to it, surrounded by a unique presence.

Briefly, I face everything I've been running away from for so long. I remember my dad, my songs. I even share some of them with my special guest.

"What's the gift behind all of this?" she asks, surrounded by the sound of birds.

"Gift?" "Behind what?"

Susan smirks as if she was waiting for this question.

> "There's this American therapist, Byron Katie, one of the therapy authors ahead of their time. She encourages us to capture destructive thoughts on paper, more specifically, formatted as questions."

---

[2] Cameron Crowe's film starring Tom Cruise, Renée Zellweger and Cuba Gooding Jr.

I look at Susan with a mix of interest in surprise.

> "It's a long process and we don't have enough time for me to explain it all to you," she continues, "but the question I asked you is the most important step in the process."

> "What's the gift behind all this?", I repeat.

I only meant to confirm if that really was the question, but she decides to answer.

> "I'm so well versed in her teachings that I've been asking myself that since the day of the first crime. There's a lot, you know? The possibility of saving lives, the meaning of the work that I love, getting to know you…"

My eyes widen, and I say:

> "Getting to know me?"

I notice that her eyes, contrary to mine, are closed.

> "You know, David, I live in a sceptical world dominated by men. If I picked fights with everyone who looked at my ass, I wouldn't have time for anything else. I work with pigs who don't feel purpose in what they do, but I don't want to believe that it was always this way. I'd like to think that they decided to put on their badges to help people, but over time got swallowed up by the system."

I dare not to interrupt her and she continues with an contagious energy you can almost feel yourself:

> "I'm not immune to this. I also saw myself start to go on autopilot. Until you showed up!"
>
> "Me?", I ask in disbelief.
>
> "I know that working in a record shop was never your dream and I can feel the energy of your purpose living deep inside you," Susan explains. "I noticed how much our search has ignited your inner flame. Like a hero, you were summoned to a mission and you accepted the call."

I turn my eyes away, until I spot the heart sculpture.

> "I haven't felt like a hero in a long time", I admit.
>
> "When we do what you did, we aren't just giving ourselves meaning, but also inspiring others."

Her words touch me in some way. I feel the urge to cry and so I close my eyes. But I keep my ears open to hear what Susan says as she continues:

"When you go to a rock show, the singer on stage doesn't tell you to follow your dreams. That would be kind of corny. However, since he's already living his life to the fullest, he end up inspiring you to aspire for the same."

She pauses before continuing:

"That's exactly what you did to me. Your passion allowed me to remember mine. I'm not part of this job to buy the expensive heels that I wear so proudly. I'm here to save lives. And that's what we're about to do now!"

The transcendental moment is abruptly and mercilessly interrupted by my phone's alarm.

It's already 6:50.

Alex will start training soon and we still need to walk over there.

He doesn't know that we're here because he didn't respond to my messages. Therefore, we should arrive before the end of practice so he has time to notice us.

We step onto the field. What an incredible sight.

My childhood friend teaches at a beautiful sports complex at Christ Church University. It's a place that mixes sports with lots of greenery. The field is perfectly cut and maintained. In the background, we spot deer, horses and oxen. The ideal ecosystem for those, like myself, who enjoy exercising and being outside.

I see Alex arrive on the field to start practice. He's already completely immersed in his work and, by how concentrated he looks, it's obvious that he loves what he does.

Practice begins and the students start warming up, running through all the basics; passing, controlling, dribbling and scoring. By the end of the drills, the ex-rocker-turned-coach is leading a well-contested team. He even choses to join in for the last few minutes which opens the floodgates to memories of our childhood.

We always asked ourselves if we'd rather try becoming football or rock stars, but although we did great with a ball at our feet, nothing compared to the magic that happened when we were together on stage.

Training's over. The sound of my friend's whistle wakes me up from my daydreams. The kids have already made their way to the lockers and my old friend is now alone on the field, gathering up the balls, cones and other sports equipment. It's the perfect time to approach him.

Susan nods to me as if to tell me I can do this one on my own. I take her advice.

Alex still hasn't noticed me yet, despite being so close to him. But from here, contrary to James, it seems like he hasn't aged a day.

Ever since our choir days, Alex had the nickname Jesus because of his hair and beard. While James had a grungier look, Alex preferred more of a hippie style, influenced by the 70s and his taste in bands like the Beatles and artists like Jimmy Hendrix.

Instead of his usual baggy, colourful clothes, he's now wearing one of the university gym uniforms. And his hair, although still long, is no longer flowing. It's trapped in a samurai-style bun. His beard, however, what was once patchy and mangy, is now impeccable. Although he hasn't necessarily changed, Alex's style has become much more refined from what it was back then.

"Alex", I say as I walk up to him. "It's been a while."

He raises his head, drops the cones that he was gathering up, looks deeply into my eyes…and books it like a defenceless child running away from a bully.

I stop in my tracks in the middle of the field, replaying the scene in my mind many times over.

But why would he do that?

He left my messages on read on Instagram, but I just thought that he might have forgotten or been busy. But running away from me as soon as he saw me…I definitely wasn't expecting this. I assume the worst and it makes me sick.

I go back to Susan to share my ideas on my friend's escape, but I find her nervously fidgeting with her phone.

> "Have you seen the news?", she says.
>
> "No."
>
> "He's already done it."
>
> "I know, we were there", I respond.
>
> "No, David." He's done it again.

What? How?

Apparently the Psycho Killer broke his pattern and has killed twice in one day.

The crime scene photos, displayed on my partner's phone, show that this victim was treated more carefully than the other. And this time the crime really did take place in the abandoned parking lot where we were stationed.

It's like he's playing with us.

But something's off about this story.

Obviously a killer doesn't have a code of conduct, but this guy loves music. And according to the news, he used *Desire* by U2. Again.

Another crime, another victim, in a different but nearby place…but also with the same song. This isn't making a lick of sense.

> "Could he have been rushed the first time and then wanted to do it again but better?" I ask. "Or could he have chosen two locations and victims just to throw us off?"
>
> "I don't think it's either of those."
>
> "Why not?"
>
> "Have you ever heard of the 'copycat effect'?"
>
> "I've heard of a film by that name…"

Susan replies to a few messages on her phone, puts it in her pocket, and turns to me to explain in better words:

> "During the time of Jack the Ripper, many other killers imitated his patterns so that they wouldn't be held accountable for their crimes. It would all fall on the serial killer's shoulders."
>
> "So you're telling me that…"
>
> "Yeah. I believe that with the dungeons case, we're dealing with a copycat. Someone who already had intentions to kill used the Psycho Killer's methods. This unfortunately ended up making us lose our footing."

While I'm stunned by the thought that someone else is capable of imitating these atrocities, I also feel deeply relieved.

I know that the Psycho Killer has to be caught and punished, but I can't hide my connection with him. I admire the way he treats the record player, the vinyl, the music as a whole…

I was disappointed by the mess that we found in the dungeon and I hope that Susan's theory is correct. It's not possible that both of today's crimes were committed by the same person. The insane mind that I've strangely learned to admire wouldn't be so careless.

But the police are going to take care of this and there's nothing we can do from here. It's better to look for Alex and complete the mission I set out to do by coming to Oxford.

Another murder happened while we were on our way here, so obviously, Alex can't be the culprit. So why did he run?

"How are we going to find your runaway friend?" asks Susan.

I think for a minute before answering:

"There's only one place he could have gone."

My friend's religious family did a good job of passing their customs on and, whenever faced with a difficult situation, my band's ex-drummer found refuge in the church. So that's where we're going.

The Christ Church Cathedral is very close to here.

We enter the sacred premises and soon after, we spot a kneeling man. The samurai bun silences any of our doubts.

I don't know if I should interrupt him or not, but Susan is faster and puts her hand on the man's shoulder.

> "Please, feel free to finish your prayers. Just don't run away after. We need to talk."

I don't know how, but Alex manages to keep his eyes closed after the not-so-subtle approach. When they finally open, my partner starts the interrogation.

> "We know you didn't do it, but why did you run?"

Although she asked him, my old friend responds while looking at me.

> "You have no idea what your abandonment at Glastonbury did to me, David. I went into a deep depression after the band broke up," he pulls down his tracksuit sleeves, but I spot the scars on wrists. "The only thing that made me want to keep living was teaching football to these kids. When I saw you, my biggest fears came back to haunt me in my place of refuge."

Disappointed in myself, I step forward and try to approach him.

"Alex, I had no idea…"

He also lowers his guard.

"I apologise for my abrupt reaction, but it was like an alarm went off inside of me. Seeing you was a trigger of that night and for everything else that haunts me the most."

I never imagined that my crisis could have caused something so serious. It's as if the world didn't punish me enough with my father's death. I also made one of my best friends suffer.

When I turn in the direction of the door, he stops me with a shy but heartfelt hug.

Enough to ease the feeling of guilt.

On the way back to London, Susan's suspicions are confirmed.

In a few hours, the police analysed the clues and identified the copycat behind the botched crime: Henry Crawford. We're talking about an amateur who not only was found in his home but also confessed to the crime.

With our copycat behind bars and the certainty that the Psycho Killer is still out there, I get a message from my former choir teacher, Mr. Boyce.

I still have some free time until then and I'm starving.

I invite Susan to stop over at my favourite pub.

I'm talking about the *Famous Cock*, a classic London Pub next to the Highbury & Islington station. We go inside, sit at a discreet table and I order the usual: Full English Breakfast. Two fried eggs, bacon, sausage, tomatoes, mushrooms, potatoes, black pudding and toast. This might sound disgusting and I'll admit that it doesn't look the most inviting, but aside from being delicious, it's also super nutritious.

To pair with it, an Irish Red Ale.

The tension of the last few hours and lack of food in our stomachs makes us devour our food in silence. When I finally take my last bite and prepare myself to exchange our first words since we arrived here, I'm interrupted.

"Hold on. I can't talk with this horrible music on."

Susan nods to the barman, who brings her her third beer in under 30 minutes. She practically downs the pint in one go and heads in the direction of the old Jukebox.

Then inserts a coin into the machine and, to everyone's content, switches the electronic music that some miserable soul put on to something more classic: *The Best* by Tina Turner.

She comes back to the table and confesses:

"Did you know that I was once part of a Tina cover band? Let me show you the pictures."

She takes out her phone from her pocket and that's when I notice the time. It's 12:20. There's only forty minutes until my meeting with the timely teacher, Mr. Boyce.

Susan's Tina Turner photos will have to wait.

I'm finally heading towards the Borough Market, a food fair near the London Bridge where the best local producers in the city are. Since I'm heading there by motorbike, I get there a few minutes earlier than we had planned, which allows me to enjoy a stroll through the delicious tents.

What brings me here is tragic, but I love this place.

Even though I'd just finished devouring a full English breakfast, the aromas in the air awakened some gastronomic memories in me.

This is where they make the best Fish n' Chips in the world and also the famous seafood wraps with scallops, shrimp and lobsters.

As I wander through my memories of other visits, I catch sight of Mr. Boyce in the corner of my eye.

It's strange. This time, we're both adults. When I was young, I was scared to death of this guy.

But it's my fault for feeling this way.

I'll never forget the time that we rehearsed the opening song of the musical *Phantom of the Opera* for weeks. Of course our reference was the original song by Andrew Lloyd Webber…but it just so happened that Iron Maiden made a rock cover version. I planned everything with Alex and James, and, on the very same day that we were going to perform the song to our parents, instead of singing the original version that I learned, I let out a vocal growl that would make Bruce Dickinson, Iron Maiden's singer, proud.

That's all it took for me to become the target of the feared Charles Boyce's persecution

Today, I understand why. He saw potential in me and wanted to put me in line so that I would be able to put anything I put my mind to.

> "Mr. Boyce", I call out to him, "You haven't aged a day."
>
> "It's nice to see you again, David."
>
> "The pleasure's all mine! It's a shame that it had to be under such circumstances."

We talk a bit about the old days and about the crimes. About how it's painful to see someone use songs that impacted our lives for something so tragic.

That's when the teacher drops a bombshell:

"But the worst of it all was discovering that the first victim was Billy's father."

"Billy? The one who always sang with us?" I ask.

"Yes, the one that followed you guys everywhere. I'd even say that he would have been part of your band if it weren't for his father…"

Of course, I remember Billy. He was a nice guy with a great ear for music.. His father took him out of the choir because he thought it was too girly. Which is absurd.

"I always had my reservations with his father," says Mr. Boyce, "but now I pity the way his life ended."

What if the killer, who already proved himself to be a big music fan, had punished Billy's dad for depriving his son of what he loved doing most?

Was that the case with all of them?

The possibility of discovering the killer's motive reignites my fire, despite not sleeping a wink last night.I head off to find Susan.

"Oh sister, I can't let you go

Like a preacher stealin' hearts at a travellin' show"

Desire - U2

Future

The young man did it.

He always dreamt of doing an acoustic show at Fellows Garden, a beautiful garden located on Magdalen College's campus, in Oxford. And now the event is about to begin, as the sun starts to set on the peaceful English city.

Only 50 lucky fans will have the privilege of attending the show.

> "Good evening, Oxford. It wasn't easy to be here today. Getting permission to play in this practically untouched garden? It's not an exaggeration to say that sacrifices needed to be made…"

The young man starts playing the first chords of *Sacrifice* by Elton John on his acoustic guitar.

Side B

Track 6

"It's a human sign

When things go wrong

When the scent of her lingers

And temptation's strong…"

Sacrifice - Elton John

Past

The father, with his hands full of a bunch of stones collected from the garden, tells the boy:

> "I'm going to make something out of these rocks. And I want to see if you can guess where we're going…"

The father arranges the stones in a circle and then puts one on top of the other.

> "I know. We're going to Stonehenge."

The boy always wanted to go see the mysterious monument with his own eyes.

Two hours is what stood between King's Cross, where they lived, and the sacred site. That's why, to make time pass by faster, the father put on one of the duo's favourite CDs:

No Guru, No Method, No Teacher by the Irish singer, Van Morrison.

Present

With my adrenaline pumping, I drive with Susan behind me and an official escort from Scotland Yard.

We're heading towards Greenwich Park, because on today's date but 1988, it was where the chart's number one song debuted in a festival.

The very song: *Sacrifice* by Elton John.

Another suggestive title.

I take my partner to the exact spot where the performance happened and we spot a warehouse nearby that stores old park chairs and tables.

Susan says she'll wait with me inside and orders the other investigators to surround the perimeter.

As soon as we enter the warehouse, we're sure that this is the perfect stage for the Psycho Killer's next crime.

The atmosphere has the same vibe as the past crime scenes, the same dark undertone…and makes my stomach churn all the same.

At 3 in the morning, we set our trap. But, although we feel a mix of nervousness and anxiety, there comes a point where we can't fight the tiredness anymore.

I think Susan notices because she then starts whispering in my ear:

"So, what's the best show you've ever been to?"

"I think this is the hardest question I could be asked, after *what's your favourite CD*."

To wake up my mind, I play along and try to come up with a solution.

I start with the legends that inspired my name. I couldn't help but consider the commemorative tour of Joshua Tree by U2, my favourite CD. Although the album is from 1987, one year before I was born, my dad listened to it in the car so much that I got hooked.

I was always frustrated by the fact that I couldn't attend this tour and I almost exploded when Bono announced that they would be doing 30-year anniversary shows. I went to all four nights that they played at the Twickenham Stadium in London.

I'm not old enough to have seen Freddie Mercury live either. But I was right in front of the stage when Queen, with Paul Rodgers on vocals, threw a concert in Hyde Park in 2016. I'm never going to forget the live version of *Under Pressure*, with a surprise appearance of David Bowie. I almost lost my mind.

But I also need to take into consideration what the Bloc Party did in 2013 at Earls Court. The energy that the vocalist, Kele Okereke instilled in the people that night was insane. The atmosphere was so electrifying that leaped into the crowd and even called some people up to join him on stage. Of course, I went up there. It happened during *She's Hearing Voices*, one of my favourite tracks of theirs.

It would be unfair to leave the Americans out, that's why I also consider Bruce Springsteen's historic concert in Wembley, in the year 2013. There's something about the mythical stadium that awakens the best in every rock star. And Bruce performed for no less than 4 hours that night, playing hits like *Dancing In The Dark* and *Thunder Road*.

But 2013 also had John Mayer's concert at Wembley Arena. It was a more intimate concert, but for someone having recently recovered from throat cancer, John was visibly moved and shared beautiful messages with the audience. To add to that, he also played *Waiting On The Day*, a super rare B-side song that I love.

I analyse each of my options, but I'm unable to come to a decision, so I list off a top 5 for Susan:

"U2 in the 30th Anniversary Joshua Tree Tour, Queen featuring Paul Rodgers in Hyde Park, Bloc Party at Earls Court, Bruce Springsteen at Wembley and John Mayer at Wembley Arena."

Judging by her expression, I think she wasn't expecting such an extended answer, but she soon after nods, expressing that she liked what she heard.

"And what about you?" I ask.

Then she tells me about a time when she was in the United States in 2016.

In Los Angeles, she watched a historic David Gilmour concert, at the Hollywood Bowl. Susan explains that the open space and the psychedelic lights on stage in addition to David's guitar playing created an unforgettable experience.

I believe every word she says.

But the story doesn't end there and so she continues:

"During this trip, I didn't plan on going to Las Vegas, especially since the last thing a police officer on vacation wants to see is a bunch of drunk people. But The Killers announced a surprise show in Sin City and I didn't hesitate: I rented a car and drove across the desert at dawn to see Brandon Flowers and co."

Susan tells me that she watched the show alone, practically pressed up against the stage, but then she discovered that, after the open show, the band would throw another closed-off concert for 100 people, in the nightclub where their career started. She took advantage of her police status to get in and ended up seeing The Killers twice in one night.

After hearing this last part, I can't mask my envy.

> "I also need to mention Bob Dylan at Wembley Arena, the same one you saw John Mayer in", continues Susan. "Just being in the same space as the living legend already makes it unforgettable."
>
> "Two to go", I comment.
>
> "Yeah."

She thinks a bit more before continuing with her top 5:

> "Do you know Death Cab For Cutie?"
>
> "Of course, it's Ben Gibbard's American indie band."
>
> "Exactly. They held a beautiful concert at Brixton Academy in 2017, and ended off with one of my favourite songs of all time: *Transatlanticism*. I was screaming like wild."

She seems to momentarily get lost in her memories.

I let her enjoy her trip down memory lane before raising my pointer finger, reminding her that she still needs to tell me about one more show.

She smiles and doesn't hesitate:

> "Lastly, a band that's also on your list, but at a different concert. U2 at the O2 Arena, the same year as yours. I already saw the band live around 10 times, but there's something about that show that moved me deeply."
>
> "So to summarise, David Gilmour, The Killers, Bob Dylan, Death Cab For Cutie and U2?" I ask.
>
> "That's it."
>
> "Not bad, huh? I didn't know that you liked music so much."
>
> "Why not? Have you already forgotten about my Tina Turner cover?"
>
> "That's right. You didn't end up showing it to me."

Susan checks her watch and looks around, checking for any signs of movement. When she doesn't detect any, she says:

> "Well, since it's just the two of us here and we have some time to kill…"

Then she starts singing quietly and I'm surprised by her control.

Enveloped by the song, I'm led somewhere deep inside me. To a place I haven't been to in a long time.

How could I keep myself away from such an innate passion for so long?

There's a killer out there, but I'm the one who killed my own dreams.

And so, united by our wish to save lives and by our love for music, Susan and I let Tina Turner's lyrics free us momentarily from our worries.

However, as soon as she finishes her excerpt, the mood changes.

It's almost time.

If we're in the right spot, the Psycho Killer will carry out his attack here any minute.

We hide ourselves in the shadows, ready to catch him in the act.

The backup team peaks in from outside of the warehouse.

The murders always happen at around 4 in the morning and the clock is about to strike the hour.

My heartbeat sounds like a double-pedal drum.

When suddenly…

> "Susan, do you hear that noise?" I ask.
>
> "Yes, it's like…like there's a concert going on outside."

We exit the warehouse and notice that all park speakers are playing an indistinguishable mix of melodies.

As if they were tuned in to multiple radio stations at the same time.

The noise is deafening.

We return to the probable scene of the crime.

Not just to wait for the killer.

But also to protect our ears.

We were only out there for a few seconds.

The Psycho Killer certainly wouldn't have enough time to set his plan into motion.

When I look around to confirm my suspicion, I see a white demonic face come out of the shadows and run towards Susan.

The figure hits my partner.

I'm next.

The second before I lose consciousness, I recognize my tormentor's disguise. His face is painted like Gene Simmons from the band Kiss.

I feel cold.

There's cold water running down my face.

I open my eyes.

Everything around me spins.

My head hurts.

Beside me, Susan rests, unconscious.

We're both handcuffed to a metal pole.

Standing in front of us is the thing that put us here. It could only be him. The Psycho Killer.

I try to reason with him, despite my pain.

Where's the backup? How did he catch us off guard? The only solution I come up with is that he had been hiding with us the whole time.

And why hasn't he killed us?

In an instant, I understand everything.

We aren't the victims.

He wants us alive.

He wants an audience for the show that's about to begin.

I tear my gaze from the killer and study our surroundings. That's when I see what's behind him, in the shadows.

The record player.

Next to it, an unconscious man. A father. A new victim.

> "Please, don't," I beg. But all I get in response is a smile on that bastard's painted face.

The Psycho Killer raises his right hand and presses a button on what seems like a remote control. Then the disturbing sound that was coming from the park speakers go completely silent.

It takes me a few seconds for my hearing to come back.

Now, instead of the noise, I hear a song.

On the record player.

Sacrifice by Elton John.

    "No," I implore, "don't do it."

He ignores me.

With theatrical gestures, as if the whole thing were some sort of twisted ballet, he picks up the vinyl record and approaches the unconscious man.

    "No," I scream, "NO."

He presses the record into the victim's neck and in one swift movement, cuts into him.

Although I try with all my might to tear out the pole or my arm from its place, my effort is in vain.

I feel the newest victim's blood hit my face. The hot, viscous liquid taints my skin, only to be washed away by my tears.

The smell of death hits me.

I roll over on all fours and throw up.

    "You bastard", I manage to whimper.

I feel disgusted with myself for having at some point saw part of myself in this psychopath.

Who goes back and puts the vinyl on the record player which takes the spotlight once again.

The executioner approaches me, very slowly. I start to think that I'll be next.

But no.

He stops a metre away from me, and bows in a way that artists typically do on stage as a gesture of gratitude.

The bastard is thanking his audience the same way a musician does after a concert.

The same way I thanked my fans.

I'm not your fan, you monster.

Helpless and useless, I watch the killer retreat and disappear into the shadows.

I don't know how many minutes go by until Susan wakes up. I don't know how many more until the police find us in a tucked away camouflaged area of the shed.

I only know that he made a fool out of us. Of all of us.

He prepared the scene, created decoys and was right under our noses the entire time.

It plays through my head like a film. *Save Me*, *Belfast Son*, *Killer*, *Heaven Is A Place On Earth*, *Desire* and *Sacrifice* make a soundtrack. Six songs for six victims. Six unique locations, from parks to churches to storage sheds.

That's more than enough. That's it. The technical police are here to do their part, but I don't want to waste another second on this search.

"Cold, cold heart

Hard done by you

Some things look better, baby

Just passing through"

Sacrifice - Elton John

I arrive at home exhausted. My body begs for rest, and although I collapse in my bed, I can't sleep. My mind's racing.

The murder I witnessed keeps replaying in my mind. Each time, I can make out the details better than the last.

The hand movements, the vinyl cutting through flesh, the blood gushing, the spasms.

I get up and take a shower. Light a cigarette. Drink a full glass of whiskey.

Nothing works.

I can't get that bastard out of my head.

I could have died tonight. Or even worse, Susan could have died too…all because she trusted me.

But that's not all.

More fathers are dying.

Every death is like mine dies all over again.

I failed him. I've failed them all.

I'm not a hero.

I'm a fraud. An imposter.

My calling isn't to save lives through music.

I need to at least be content in at least saving my own.

That's it.

I was getting better. I had a fixed job, good habits, and a routine. I need to regain the stability that I'd built.

I look outside and already see the sun high in the sky. I check the clock and do a quick mental calculation.

I put on a coat and leave, heading to the Rough Trade, to the job that I simply abandoned to go serial killer hunting.

When Pamela gets there to open the store, I'm already there with a cup of coffee in my hands. She widens her eyes like she'd seen a ghost and then looks at her feet.

> "Hi", I say awkwardly.

> "Hi," she replies also with a certain awkwardness about her. "There's an envelope for you inside."

I open it. It's a letter. I'm fired.

Given the circumstances, I'd consider them even generous. They gave me a small severance pay, asked me to take care of myself and to get my life back on track.

Humiliated, I wander haphazardly around London until I decide to walk into the first pub I come across. Maybe the right amount of Irish Red Ales will make the feeling of shame go away.

My telephone rings several times, and with each new ring, I ignore it and order another pint of beer.

Sorry, Susan, but I can't today.

When I'm hitting the right buzz, I see her enter through the pub's front doors with a few new friends and heads over in my direction.

>"How did you find me?" I ask.

>"I'm a police officer, remember?" says Susan, her eyebrows pulling together. "What do you think you're doing?"

I raise my pint of Red Ale.

>"Get up", she says.

>"No, Susan, I'm out."

>"Get up, I'm not going to let that asshole do this to you."

I tip the glass and down the red liquid in a single gulp.

>I need some peace. "I need to sleep", I explain.

But she doesn't seem to agree with my wishes and lifts me up by my arm, almost dragging me away from the table.

> Get up, because it's thanks to you that we've discovered something important.

I feel my despair leave me almost immediately. I stand up strong, and look in her direction.

That's when she explains to me that the police spoke to Billy, the one from my childhood choir. The same Billy who had his father murdered by the Psycho Killer.

> "And what did they find out?", I ask.
>
> "He said that he quit music because of his father," says Susan. "That his father never believed in a future in music and that his son should pursue a more traditional career."
>
> "I was right," I conclude.
>
> "Yeah, more than you think."

Susan tells me that the police spoke with the children of the other victims and it seems like they were hearing different accounts of the same story.

One loved music, but their father said that it wouldn't make any money.

Another had a dream of becoming a rock star, but his father said it was devil's work.

Another always wanted to have a band, but his step-father made him take over the family business.

"We have a motive," says Susan. "We already know what makes him kill."

"Ok, so now what?"

"There must be millions of frustrated musicians with parents like this in England. I need to understand how the Psycho Killer chooses his victims out of this select group of people."

I dare not say anything. I just look at the police officer.

"I can't do this without you, David," she says, finally. "Please, help me."

Future

> "I always wanted to hold a show here. I thought it was impossible, but in 2018 my friend Paul Oakenfold got permission to do it."

The young man tunes his guitar on stage in the middle of Stonehenge.

> "Paul, with all due respect to your electronic music, but this here is an arena made for rock and roll."

The audience cheers and applauds, making the young man smile before continuing:

> "My Dad loved this singer. And since we're staged in a place like this, I'm going to have to start off by saying that *the fields are always wet with rain…*"

Then he gives it his all as he sings the first verses of the song *In The Garden* by Van Morrison.

Side B

Track 7

"You wiped the teardrops from your eye in sorrow

Yeah we watched the petals fall down to the ground

And as I sat beside you, I felt the great sadness that day

In the garden…"

In The Garden - Van Morrison

Past

The father wakes up the boy, whispering in his ear:

"I have some good news and some bad news."

"Start with the good news," responds the boy, already sitting up tall in his bed.

"Today our car ride will take 6 hours. 3 to get there and 3 to come back."

The boy smiles wide hearing the news.

"Yay! The more, the better. I'm going to pick out the CD's…"

"That's the bad news…"

The child's smile turns into confusion.

"What do you mean, bad news?"

"No CD's today."

"So what are we going to do for six hours?"

Now it's the dad's turn to smile.

"We're going to sing," he says.

"Sing?", questions the boy, worried, "but I don't know how…"

"I think you're old enough to start learning. Also, I want to show you some old songs I composed."

The child's curiosity seems to speak louder than his worry, which dissolves almost immediately.

"Okay, Dad. And where are we going?"

"Glastonbury."

"Wait, but isn't the festival only in the summer?"

"It is, but that place has a magical energy about it," says the father.

The man then looks up and seems to be staring at something only he can see. After letting out a sigh, he shares his prophecy:

"Who knows, it may even inspire you to play there one day

Present

I had researched the nuances of the probable murders up to *Sacrifice* by Elton John. My hope was that at this point, the Psycho Killer would have already been captured, but he proved to be much more intelligent and cruel than anyone could have imagined.

Susan stops the car at a convenience store for a well-deserved break between visiting the children of each victim. To make the most of our break, I think about the next crime.

If I'm not mistaken, the song that topped the charts on this exact day in 1988 is *In The Garden* by Van Morrison. My father's biggest Irish idol and fellow countryman.

I take note of this information on a piece of paper and scan the area in search of Susan. She's waiting in a huge queue, which gives me some more time to think about where the first song was played.

This time, it's not difficult to find the answer because the memories come flooding back.

"It was at the Glastonbury festival in 1988," I say to myself out loud.

The Psycho Killer's next victim will be murdered on the same stage that I refused to go on.

A few days ago, my life was like any other. I was dusting off some vinyls at work. Then, one news story changed everything. Will things ever go back to normal one day?

But is it normal to work in a shop like a zombie every day?

Is there anything normal about locking your dreams away in a safe?

Strange as it may seem, the crimes have brought me closer to my biggest passion, as if it were a calling, an awakening. And the world is showing me in the most terrible way possible that you can't hide from your purpose.

I ignored my musicality for years and if it weren't for a certain rock n' roll psychopath, I'd still be on auto-pilot, running away from my talents and the mission that was given to me to use them.

I was wasting my life…and how many people out there are doing the exact same thing?

The thought scares me, but also instigates a new commitment.

It took a series of deaths to reconnect me with music. I had to learn from the pain. I can't throw away this knowledge. I need to honour all of these sacrifices.

Every one of these father's lives must have meant something.

My father's, too.

I'm snapped out of this line of thought by the sound of the car door opening. It's Susan, armed with coffee and some snacks that will be what appeases our hunger for the next hours to come.

The car's clock reads midnight. We wanted more time to try to find some kind of pattern in the children's explanations, but we'll have to sort this out on the way, since London is the next probable crime scene and it's a 3-hour drive from here.

I try to get some sleep on the ride over, like I did as a child in my dad's car. But I'm unable to relax. My mind is racing with a thousand questions and few answers.

Who will be the chosen one? Is Glastonbury proof that I'm really stuck in the middle of this mess?

We already know that the killer targets men in their 60s. And that these men somehow prevented their children from following their passion for music. But, among all the fathers who have done this, how am I going to know which one it's going to be this time?

My questions are interrupted by a nudge from Susan. She points to the radio and turns up the volume.

> "Do you like my playlist?"

She asks me just as the first chords of *Show Me How To Live* by Audioslave start to play - which, in my opinion, is one of the greatest road trip songs of all time.

"Yeah, I like it a lot. The chorus…"
"I know. I made the playlist with you in mind," she says. "Having worked years in this line of work, I've been hardened with experience, but I can't even begin to imagine how you're holding up with all of this."

She holds the silence for a few moments longer, letting Chris Cornell's voice fill the vehicle. Then she concludes:

"I know it's difficult, but try to relax. We're going to need you and all your strength to face this monster."

I lean back in my seat and close my eyes, at least resting my body.

As I listen to her selected music, I start to feel moved by my partner's kindness and the bond we've built throughout this crisis. U2, Bruce Springsteen. Queen, Bob Dylan…she literally made this playlist for me.

It's been so long since I've felt the fresh breeze on my face mixed with rock and roll's electricity. And when I'm almost lost in a trance while listening to *Run* by Snow Patrol, I'm pulled back to reality.

"We're almost there," says Susan.

I look around. The clear skies of the past few days have now become drizzly, with cold rain. A shift in weather that could only be expected in London. Now all that surrounds us is pitch-black darkness of the night and brown mud.

We stop the car.

I open the door and my boot squishes into the wet ground.

The feeling transports me directly to the memories of the worst night of my life. One that could have brought me closer to my dream but instead became a nightmare.

I remember every detail.

Arriving with my band members and their families. Our smiles, walking backstage... And the moment that changed everything. The exact moment where my happiness turned to panic.

It's impossible to forget my father's futile attempt to snap me out of it. And the last words I said to him.

Unfortunately, the image of every beer I drank to numb the emptiness that morning is also as clear as day.

And while I was busy doing that, my dad drowned himself in the Thames River.

The guilt eats at me.

If I had been there with him, would he have been more careful? Did he drink before driving? Could I have prevented it?

"And then one day you came back home

You were a creature all in rapture

You had your key to your soul

And you did open that day you came back to the garden"

In The Garden - Van Morrison

- Hey, wake up!

Susan brings me back to reality.

We head to the Pyramid Stage dressing rooms, where the Van Morrison Show in 1988 was held, and today's probable crime scene location.

Since the festival is outdoors, we manage to see some crows flying around while standing under the roofed area protecting us from the rain.

I've already been here many times in my life, as a fan. On show days, the atmosphere is so lively, with people packing the floor. But empty like this, the sight is quite sombre.

Time passes surrounded by this bad omen.

I don't know if I do this to fill the silence, for being in this place again or for some other motive that I'm not capable of understanding, but I reveal my trauma to Susan in detail.

"What was the setlist of your show going to be like?", she asks.

Susan is great at easing the tension and inviting us to a calmer space. Which is exactly what she's doing now.

I notice her efforts and accept her invitation.

"We were going to play 10 of our songs from our first album and a few covers," I say.

"You never told me about your songs. Which one was your favourite?"

I chuckle quietly, which comes out more through my nose than my mouth.

"Answering this is like trying to choose your favourite child," I confess. "But I have three songs that I'm really proud of: *It Starts With Pain*, *The Search* and *Gran Finale*. Each of them are about finding your purpose in life. The first one invites you to understand your pain and find meaning in it. The second, an attempt to transform your pain into something positive. While the third one–"

"Sing a part of the first one for me?" she asks.

My first impulse is to turn her down.

But my body seems to rebel against my dark and fearful feelings, suddenly I'm closing my eyes and taking a deep breath.

My heart beats fast and each thump echoes through every molecule of my being.

I haven't sung these lines since the night that ended my life.

Maybe it's time to go back to living.

I take another deep breath and then my voice breaks free:

"Why do I get up?

Why do what I do?

Why fill the cup?

Why break the taboo?

Why do I pray?

For some love.

Blue or grey.

As skies above.

Why do I try?

Why meditate?

Why do I cry?

Or instead celebrate?

It Starts With Pain - The Sunflowers

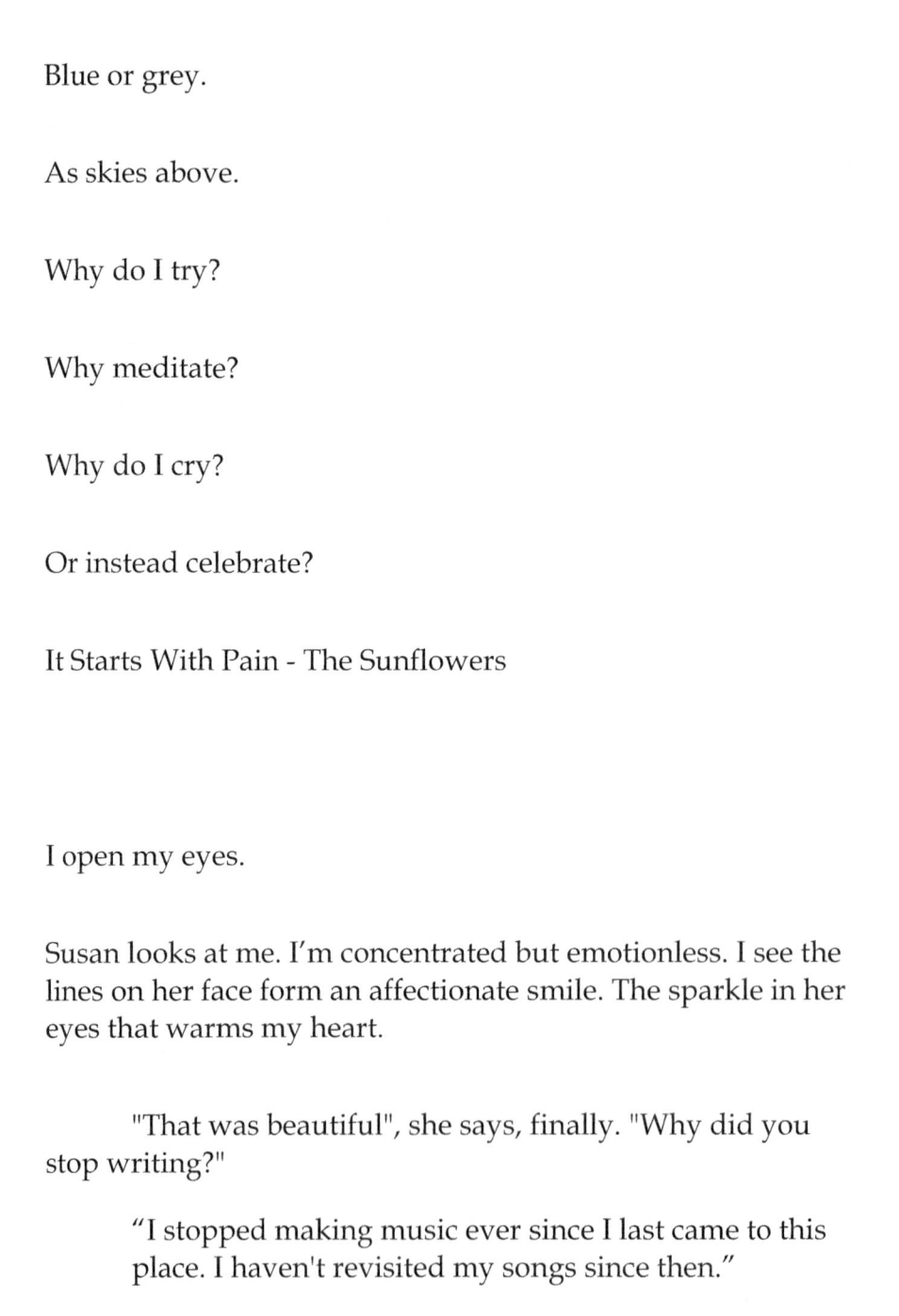

I open my eyes.

Susan looks at me. I'm concentrated but emotionless. I see the lines on her face form an affectionate smile. The sparkle in her eyes that warms my heart.

"That was beautiful", she says, finally. "Why did you stop writing?"

"I stopped making music ever since I last came to this place. I haven't revisited my songs since then."

I look around, noticing every detail of the place that's haunted me so much over the past few years.

"I can't help but wonder what my life would have been like if I hadn't run away," I say. "At the time, I thought that I was going to die, but what's the worst that could have happened? I sing badly, the crowd boos at me, but who cares? I had the chance to follow my dream, my passion, but most of all...my dad would still be here..."

Susan lets me stand in silence for a few moments. The silence breaks only a few minutes after, when she sings the verses of *Starts With Pain* and we attempt to duet it.

We speak a little more. I sing *The Search* and *Gran Finale* until she memorises the lyrics of these two as well. But, over the course of singing, we realise that the unwanted hour is upon us.

Once again, she was able to make the tense and anxious moments of waiting fly by. Regardless of what happens, getting to know her has been a blessing.

It's 3:47 in the morning.

Adrenaline eliminates any of my lingering drowsiness. We're alert for any sign of movement. Our team is on standby. It has to be today.

The minutes tick by. It's already almost 4 in the morning, when the crimes usually happen. Up until now, there hasn't been any sign of the criminal.

We wait.

There's no way that the Psycho Killer is behind schedule.

We check the news. There's been no sign of any other killing.

4:32. Susan calls it.

> "That's it. Serial killers don't stray from their rituals."

And with that, we leave.

Susan calls off the standby and I walk to the car feeling conflicted. I'm relieved because nobody died today, but also disappointed because I thought we'd catch the psychopath.

I came to this traumatic place for nothing, I think.

I take my first step towards the car lot.

I can't take the second.

> "Susan, I need to make one last stop before we go."

Future

The young man finally is back on the stage where everything started:

"I think I owe you all this show for a few years now, right?"

Side B

Track 8

"In the end, it all makes sense

The words you spoke

The blood you spilled

Can you see it now?

Oh, can you see it now?

Gran Finale - The Sunflowers

Past

On the way back home, the father asks the boy:

> "And? Did you like seeing the sacred rock temple?"
>
> "I did, Dad. But I have to confess that it's prettier in the photos than like this, empty and full of mud."

The father guffaws.

> "Yes, son, that's true," he says, "but the most important thing is the energy."
>
> "I'm kidding, Dad, I loved it."

The boy pauses for a few seconds, gathering the courage to state his revelation:

> "Can I tell you something? I felt that one day I'll sing there."

Present

Susan was nice enough to let me borrow her car and she got a ride back with the police. She understood that I have to face my demons here and I need to do so alone.

I walk to the alternative tent's backstage, where I had my panic attack that altered the course of my life. Curiously enough, I'm wearing an outfit that's very similar to the one I was wearing on that fateful day: a leather jacket and boots, jeans and a white shirt.

Taking the last steps before entering the dressing room, I relive every moment of that night.

Chills go up my spine and I can almost hear our music playing.

The absence of rest over the past few days gives me the feeling that I'm never 100% awake. It's like I'm in limbo, in a constant state of numbness, which makes it difficult for me to distinguish fiction from reality.

Am I daydreaming?

I get closer. I'm in the exact spot where I had the conversation with my father.

The sound gets louder.

I can see the back part of the stage and I notice there's something there. I approach it.

It's a record player. In perfect condition. Playing our album. Playing my song, *Starts With Pain*.

I shouldn't, but I take a few more steps forward. Since I had to come and face the ghosts of my past, I'm going to confront them all.

It's all set up. The instruments are in their positions. There's even an old banner hung up in the background, with "The Sunflowers" written on it in big letters.

What's happening?

My biggest nightmare is right in front of me. The worst day of my existence, perfectly recreated.

I feel myself drawn into the microphone. A mysterious power possesses me. A feeling that only those who have performed in front of an audience can understand.

I start singing.

As I sing through the first verses, I see someone approaching me. The lighting on the stage blocks out my vision and I can't identify the man that's walking up to me in my direction.

"Sing, David," he says.

I recognize his voice.

"What is the end after all?

Is it when you finally rise?

Or when you just fall?"

The End - The Sunflowers

Sing, David.

This is exactly what James Edgard would say to me every time a show was about to start. He's the one standing in front of me now.

James leans against the stage, but doesn't invite himself up, like a devoted fan.

"Sing, David," he says again.

"James, what are you doing here?"

"I came here to see you do what you do best. I came here to see you reunite with your destiny…"

He pauses briefly and the corner of his mouth pulls into a grin before continuing:

"I came here to help you finally follow your purpose in life."

But how? How did you know I would be here? And exactly at this time?

Unless…the murders…

My mind lights up with a terrible conclusion.

"Sing, David."

I can't even open my mouth. I'm in shock, paralysed on stage.

"Everything started back then, remember?" he asks. "It was the best day of my life. I would have achieved my…no, not mine…*our* dream."

James walks in front of the stage. His eyes look distant, as if he could see a projected image of that night so many years ago, when I failed everyone who believed in me.

> "One show in Glastonbury would have introduced us to the world and changed our band's trajectory, David. We were ready to make a living with music. And make a good living, at that," he continues. "I finally would have proven my dad wrong. Until yours interfered with the story."

What? What the hell is James talking about?

> "I'm never going to forget how he made you give up on everything. It happened right in front of me. He was holding you, shaking you, convincing you to stop."

That's not what happened.

> "James, it wasn't…", I try to say.
>
> "I get it, DJ," he looks at me. "My old man did the same thing to me. You were already far away from us, probably drinking away your sorrows, but after we didn't go up on stage, the bastard who brought me into this world gave me the biggest beating of my life."

James runs his hand over his face, revealing some of the scars around his upper lip and left eyebrow.

> "Do you see these scars?" he says. "I wear them not only in my soul but on my body, to this day."
>
> "My god. I didn't know that…"
>
> "Don't worry about it, mate. He can't bother us anymore."

And with that answer, he smiles. Revealing a frightening detail.

> "James, what did you do?" I dare to ask.
>
> "On the night that you ran away from your mission, I discovered mine. Through experiencing so much pain, as shown in the music that's playing now, I felt it in my bones that I was put on this world to prevent fathers like ours from destroying their children's dreams. This gave my entire existence meaning."

Without realising it, I raise my hand to cover my mouth, horrified by the reality that is slowly being revealed to me.

My bandmate…my friend…he's a psychopath.

Like a villain from a superhero movie, James starts talking. I think he needs this. To get it all off his chest. He makes a point of it that I need to know every detail about his motives behind everything and what made him who he is today. In his mind, he is right. He sees himself as the hero of this story.

He explains how, on that morning, after being beaten by his father, he waited for the man to drown himself in whisky and pass out in the car. Then he got into the car, not fully knowing what to do, until he saw, thrown on the car floor, a sample of our vinyl record.

> "It was a work of fate, David. Practically a message for me," he says. "Right then and there, with that vinyl, I was reborn."

"When I look inside

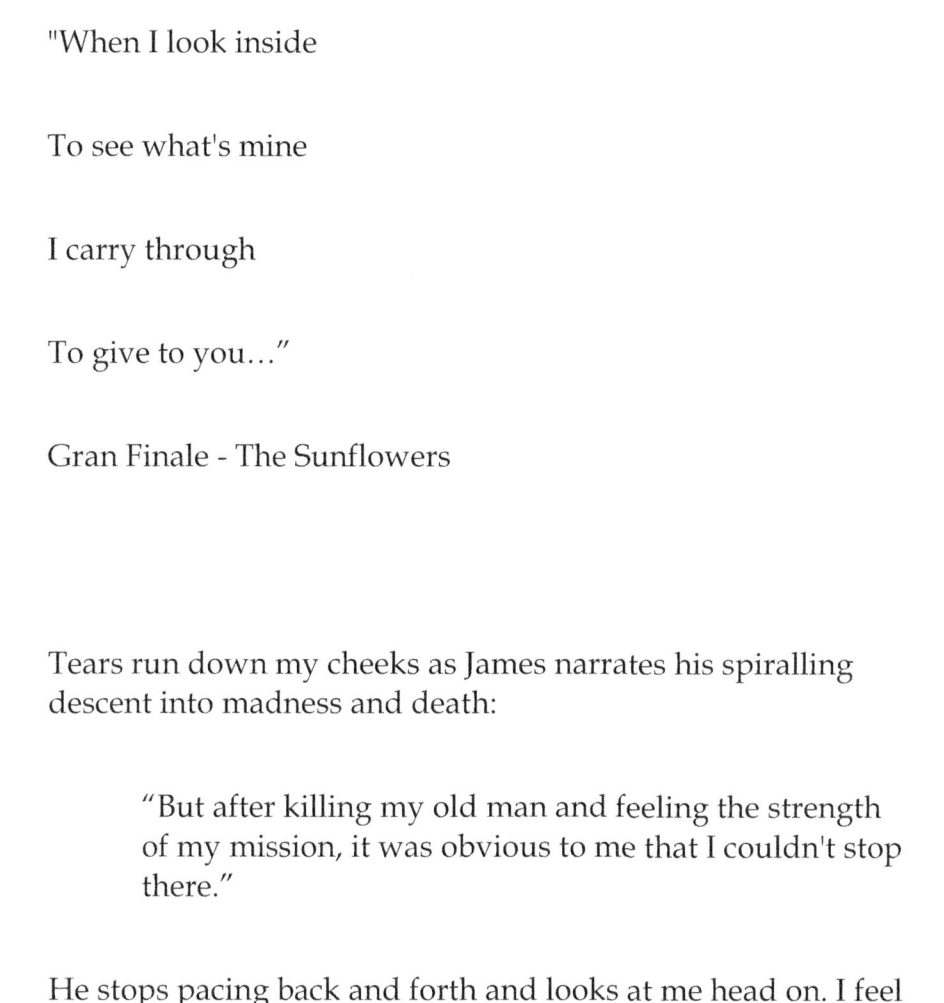

To see what's mine

I carry through

To give to you…"

Gran Finale - The Sunflowers

Tears run down my cheeks as James narrates his spiralling descent into madness and death:

> "But after killing my old man and feeling the strength of my mission, it was obvious to me that I couldn't stop there."

He stops pacing back and forth and looks at me head on. I feel all the intensity of his stare, of his madness and of the twisted purpose he's taken on.

> "The Psycho Killer," he says mockingly. "I was never a fan of the Talking Heads song, but I eventually got used to this name they've given me."

I wanted to do something besides cry, but I have no idea what to say.

I'm lifeless, shaken, like a child face to face with the monster that terrorises their dreams.

> "Don't you understand, David? We came into this world with a defined goal, a task to be accomplished."

Then he explains to me in a soothing voice that my mission was to save lives through music. While his is to make sure that nobody stops musicians from doing so. That's why he gives music theory classes, because he can better understand which parents are like his and stop their kids from shining.

> "But not under my watch," he concludes proudly. "Not after I finish my work."

Every hair on my body stands on end. My survival instincts say that I should run far away from here as fast as I can and never look back. But I can't do this.

Maybe part of my soul is tired of running, maybe part of me yearns to put an end to the silent despair that my life has become. That's why I don't leave the stage.

I stand my ground while I listen to James tell me that today is the day of my final act.

While he explains how he meticulously set up this stage and the consequences of our meeting.

> "Dave, have you ever thought about what your death will do for our album?"

I'm terrified, confused and heartbroken, but my mind still struggles to make any sense of it all.

My childhood best friend and bandmate is the Psycho Killer. He killed his own father and all the victims over the past few weeks. Besides that, he thinks that he's doing good by eliminating everyone who stops their children from singing.

And now he wants to kill me as a sacrifice to revive the band and leave a message that will be passed on to the world.

> "Dave, it's time for you to do your part for the band that you didn't do the last time we were here."

Now he finally gets up on stage.

> "The night is yours. It's your turn to show your work to the world," he says. "To show everyone what happens when we let go of our passion."

James takes slow, light steps in my direction.

> "Today, you leave behind your life. And I'll leave behind the Psycho Killer."

The last sentence snaps me out of it.

"What?" I ask. "What do you mean?"

"Through your example, everyone will understand that it's impossible to abandon our gifts. Once this message is out there, my work wouldn't be necessary anymore," he explains. "Your existence and my killings end today, together."

So that's it. He's telling me that he's going to stop after tonight. That, with my collaboration, nobody else will need to get hurt.

"Now sing, David."

I obey.

Because I don't know what else to do. To buy time. For thinking that this might be the best way to stop this nightmare.

God knows why, but I sing.

I grab the microphone, close my eyes and start chanting the first words of *Starts With Pain*.

When I reach the highest notes, James applauds:

"Bravo. Bravo."

I open my eyes and see that he's holding our vinyl record in his hands, cleaning it affectionately.

I know the ritual.

He's preparing my murder.

Even so, I can't stop singing and instead I reflect on his words. That his work ends now.

I also think about my dream of saving lives through music.

If I let him take me as a sacrifice, isn't that exactly what I'll be doing?

My death could prevent several others.

And isn't that a trade worth making?

I could leave this world as a hero, instead of as a useless coward that can't even keep his job in a record shop. With the repercussions of the murder, my album will probably hit the top of the charts, repaying my debts to my former band members. But more importantly, other victims would be spared.

Was this the outcome the Gods wrote for me? That everything that happened was just for me to be faced with this choice?

Maybe all the horrors of my last visit to this stage was necessary for us to reach this point.

Maybe this is a way for me to bring justice to my father's death.

I abandoned him that night. I lost the one I loved the most. Now I can reconnect with my dad and prevent other children from suffering through the same pain.

My head lightens and I feel a peace that I hadn't felt since I would rock out on stage. It's as if I were hypnotised. By the microphone, by music. Suddenly the world seems to make sense and all the pain and doubts that I carried inside me are silenced at once.

I also calm myself down.

James approaches me. He holds me gently by the arm and leads the way.

In one of his hands he holds a tranquilliser syringe, it's how he knocked out all his other victims, but he decides to put it back in his jacket pocket.

"I'm not going to need this, right?" he asks.

I shake my head to say no, no you won't.

My friend and executioner sits me down in the same position as all the other deaths. I know, I saw them. Only now, it's my turn.

I closely observe the routine that I've been obsessing over these past few days.

James puts the record player in its usual place and picks up the vinyl the same way someone would hold a weapon. In his hands, that's what it's become.

I'm going to be killed by my band's vinyl record. I'm going to die for my music. Literally. The scene is set.

I can already imagine the cover of tomorrow's newspaper:

David June, yet another Psycho Killer victim.

I hope it's the last.

> "You have to promise me that this is the last time", I say

James puts his hand on my shoulder, in an unusual display of affection.

> "That was always the plan, David. Everything I did was for this purpose: to make you reconnect with your greatest talent. And now we're going to inspire others to do the same."

I nod with my head, accepting my tragic fate, but James still has more to say:

> "I knew that the songs from 1988 would speak to you. I thought that you would start to put together the connection between the songs and the murders. I always knew that we'd end up again in this stage. You will meet your end here. As will the Psycho Killer. My goal will be achieved. With the news of your murder, our album will rise to the top. Our band will become eternal. The world will understand that we can't abandon our destinies. Nobody else will need to suffer. I will continue our legacy. The character I am today was created here, on the day that our parents deprived us from following our paths. And today, at the same place, I will abandon it forever."

In a sick way, it all makes sense. Except for one small detail:

James said that our parents deprived us from following our paths, but…

> "My father never deprived me of anything", I say.
>
> "You don't have to lie to me, Dave. I saw him holding you. Preventing you from getting on stage. I know that he was the one responsible for your panic attack."

No. My dad was trying to motivate me. Help me overcome my fears. He was always my biggest motivator. If he were still alive, I probably would have got back into singing.

I summon up the courage to ask the inevitable question.

"James, what happened to my dad?"

"What matters now is that they won't hold us back from anything anymore and, after your grand sacrifice, no one else will dare to try to do the same."

Then all the passive acceptance that had overcome me is swept away, giving way to an immense fury that bursts out of me in a form of a scream:

"What happened to my dad?"

"It hurts to stare

At the eye of the beast

It's hard to compare

To say the least…"

Gran Finale - The Sunflowers

James confesses:

"Look, after discovering my purpose, I couldn't leave my friend hanging out to dry."

He tells me about how he waited for my father in the parking lot. How he asked for a ride home and how he took his vinyl records with him.

> "At one point, your father stopped at a stop sign. He closed his eyes and tilted his up, as if he were speaking with the heavens. At that moment, I understood. It was another sign. Another exposed throat, right in front of me."

I feel my body burning up. I'm a pressure cooker about to explode and I think James notices this.

He grabs me by the shoulders and shakes me, trying to force his explanation into my head.

> "He didn't want you to go up on stage, Dave. He killed your career. There's nothing more fair than dying through your art," he gets up, clearly nervous. "Even I thought that after his death, you'd sing again, but from what I can tell, his words oppressed you too much. I noticed that many other fathers did the same. That's why I couldn't stop. But today, after we present our final work, I can. You can. Let's make history and finally rest."

I walk towards him and grab him by his shirt:

"Where is my dad?", I scream at him.

He points somewhere in the distance.

"Not very far from here, along with mine."

To my deep disgust and sadness, James reveals how he hid our dad's bodies in my father's old Mustang. He explains how he waited until the end of the festival to bury them in a field close to the stage where we would have played. And then he finishes his story off by explaining how he drove the car into the river, after damaging the breaks, to make them think that it was an accident.

Monster.

James is a monster who only sees darkness. And I was almost convinced by him to give up my life so that he would end his killings.

Now I understand.

He won't stop.

The Psycho Killer will find an excuse to kill again.

An unjustified reason, an insane message that only makes sense to him.

And that's why I can't allow it.

My first impulse is to punch him. And add some more scars to his collection. But I remember the tranquilliser in his pocket.

Also, I don't know if I'm strong enough to subdue James in a fight. If I lose, I'll be dead and he'll get away again.

I won't solve this through violence. Violence was never my strong suit.

Instead, I go with another option:

"James, can I make one last request?" I ask. "Could we play together one last time?"

"One…last time?" he repeats, touched, his voice faltering.

We plug in the instruments.

I start playing the chords of *Gran Finale*.

My band member and rival joins in.

We put on the show we should have on this very stage, the day my life fell apart.

And, unfortunately, I'm going to have to tear my old friend and now killer's life apart, too.

After one minute of playing together, I use the most destructive weapon of all.

The one a songwriter can always count on:

Words.

> "Play it right, you fairy."

That's exactly what James' dad would tell him, right before he would get abusive and violent.

I notice James' expression changes to shock and disbelief.

> "David, what…"

"Play like a man, you piece of shit," I say even more aggressively. "Play this shit right."

He takes a few steps back and plays the music completely wrong.

> "David, I'm sorry, I…"

I don't give him the room to recover. I move forward with an increasingly wild and ruthless spirit.

I'm never going to forget about the day I attended a rehearsal at the Edgards' house and heard all the swearing that eventually turned into a beating. I promised myself I'd never do the same to my son and today I'm embodying it.

But it's necessary.

> "You made me come all the way here so that you would play it wrong? Focus on this shit, or I'll beat the shit out of you!"

James falls to his knees, babbling meaningless excuses. His face, once so frightening, turns into a mess of tears and saliva that pours out of his trembling lips.

Even knowing that he's a cruel killer, the scene is hard to watch.

> "Do you think you're special? That you won't have to work like me? That rock and fucking roll will take you places?" I scream at the top of my lungs. "You really are a spoiled little shit."

He throws himself on the ground, begging me to stop. Begging his father to forgive him.

But I continue:

> "Sorry for what? I didn't even want you to be born. Your mum didn't want to do anything about it and now here I am supporting a deadbeat son."

James curls into a foetal position, like a baby who wants his mother. And that's exactly who he cries out for.

> "Mum, help me, mum!"

The dreaded Psycho Killer is screaming, defeated, at the mercy of his deepest traumas.

He's so shaken that he doesn't even notice me taking the syringe out of his pocket. And he doesn't even try to pull away from the needle that I inject into his arm.

The killer that shocked London is so lost in his personal hell that he only stops crying when the tranquilliser takes effect and he passes out.

I take a few steps back, still standing on stage, admiring the scene. Then I take out my phone and with one call, I lift the weight of the world off my shoulders.

>"Susan, we won."

Future

In front of the crowd, the young man confesses.

> "Only my father knew about this, but the day I failed to come up to this stage wasn't my first time at Glastonbury."

The whole crowd holds their breath, as if they're preparing to take in every one of his next words:

> "When I was a kid, my old man brought me here, on a rainy non-festival day, just for me to feel the energy. It worked. Since then, I always dreamed of coming back and showing you the purpose that dominates my heart."

While the crowd applauds enthusiastically, the young man pauses to wipe away his tears. He takes a deep breath and starts to play the last song of the night.

Side B

Encore

Past

Still on the road, heading the way back home and thrilled by the boy's declaration that he wants to sing on the Glastonbury stage one day, the father reveals:

> "Ah, is that so? Then I'm going to ask you one thing: when I was a little older than you are now, I started writing a song. If one day you go up on that stage, do you promise to sing it for me?"

Present

We got the Psycho Killer, but I'm still not at peace.

While we're returning from Glastonbury to London, I not only reflect on what happened in my life recently, but also on how I should live from here on out.

James commented that all he did was get me back in touch with my mission. I feel like, although his means were of the worst possible kind, he was kind of right

I was avoiding facing my destiny. I was hiding in a record store, unhappy and praying for the time to go by faster.

I can't go back to that.

It's true that, before all this, my habits were better, my health was better and, in some ways, I was even more mature. But life's not just about that. There needs to be a balance. It takes the flame ignited from something else, added to the comfort of a routine.

Six people died for me to understand this.

Lives were lost so that I would stop wasting mine…I hope that you don't need that much of a push.

Now I see that, although we may falter and hide, our dreams don't give up on us.

I clearly see what the universe brought us here with a role to fulfil.

We can try to mask it or numb it…but none of that helps.

Nothing but purpose will fill the voids in our chests. The thing we were born to follow.

At the top of this epiphany, the answer strikes me like lightning.

I know exactly what to do.

The solution is to not go back to an irresponsible life that revolves around nights out, drinks and music. These habits never got me anywhere.

It's also not risking it all to pursue my dreams. That's what the Psycho Killer did and look where that vision took him.

It's also not trading my dreams and passions for an ordinary routine just because I have to act like an adult and pay the bills.

No.

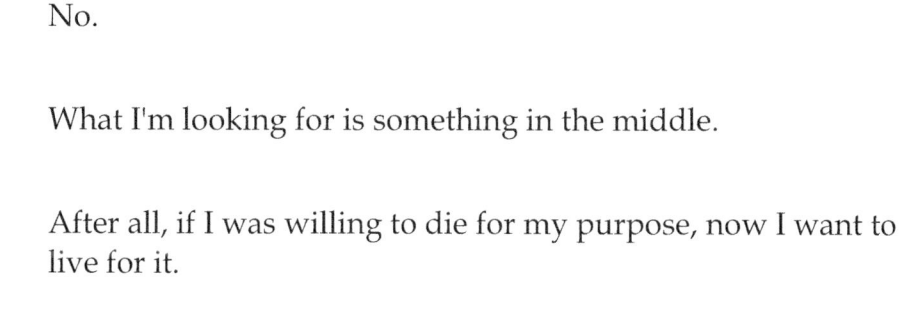

What I'm looking for is something in the middle.

After all, if I was willing to die for my purpose, now I want to live for it.

Life after the Psycho Killer's arrest takes a new turn, reconnecting with the best parts of my old self with my new habits.

The training, meditation and cold showers will continue. But I went back to riding my motorbike, and wearing my leather boots and jacket.

Cigarettes and bacon? Things of the past. But there's always a small stock of Red Ales in the fridge for special occasions.

To make things better, I keep playing and singing like never before.

I leave my home early with my destination ready, well away from the record store.

I drive fast and safe, with the same urgency as someone who has important things to do. After all, aside from fatherless children, Jamees left many students without a teacher. But not anymore. It's time to keep saving people through music.

I introduce myself in the school where he used to teach called *Getting In Tune*, named after the famous song by "The Who". The director is waiting for me.

"Hello, Director Benjamin", I say.

"You can call me Ben," he replies. "But what should I call you? Rock Star?"

"Ah, director…I mean, Ben…I wouldn't say I play well enough to deserve that name."

"I'm not the one calling you that."

He throws the newspaper in my direction. I grab it in the air, open it to the first page and read:

Rock Star Captures Psycho Killer. Meed David June, the musician who helped capture James Edgard and now sits at the top of the UK charts…

Future

After wiping the tears from his face on the main stage of the biggest festival in England, the young man continues:

> "On our way back home, my old man sang the first lines of this song to me. I promised him that one day I'd introduce it to the world. Dad, wherever you are, this one's for you…"

Still moved and accompanied by his fans, David June finishes off his first show in Glastonbury with the hit song *Gran Finale*, composed by him and his father.

Epilogue

In the gardens of the HMP Belmarsh prison, in the south-east region of London, it's leisure time for the inmates.

While one of them tries to lift weights, the other whistles a song while flipping through the newspaper.

"Hey, could you stop making that racket? I'm trying to concentrate here."

The tune doesn't stop, so the body builder drops his weights, gets up and approaches the whistler.

"Oh, it's you...you don't seem so tough in here without your mask and records. Am I going to have to make you shut up?"

He doesn't reply, but instead starts to whistle louder, in the rhythm of *Gran Finale*.

The thug starts to feel irritated, especially when he sees a smile creep up the corner of James Edgard's face, the killer who became a celebrity.

> "Let's see that smile after I do this."

He snatches the news from his fellow inmate's hands and throws the pages on the ground. However, even crumpled, it's still possible to read the main headline:

Rock Star Captures Psycho Killer. Meed David June, the musician who helped capture James Edgard and now sits at the top of the UK charts…

The inmate looks at James, puzzled.

> "Why are you smiling? Don't you know how to read? Don't you understand? Now you're in hell, man."

James stands up, still smiling. The same one that he kept hidden under his mask right before he was about to kill.

Then, with all the calmness in the world, the Psycho Killer responds:

> "Hell is not living out your purpose…"

Author's Note

Art allows us to access teachings that aren't explicitly stated.

A good work of fiction should be like this:

Learning disguised as entertainment.

You're reading, unpretentiously being entertained, when suddenly…

That's it!

You discover a long sought-after truth.

That's the writer's role.

To leave hidden messages between the lines.

Translate and communicate these pearls of wisdom.

So that those who read them feel a sense of acceptance and belonging.

Anything that surpasses this is justifiable.

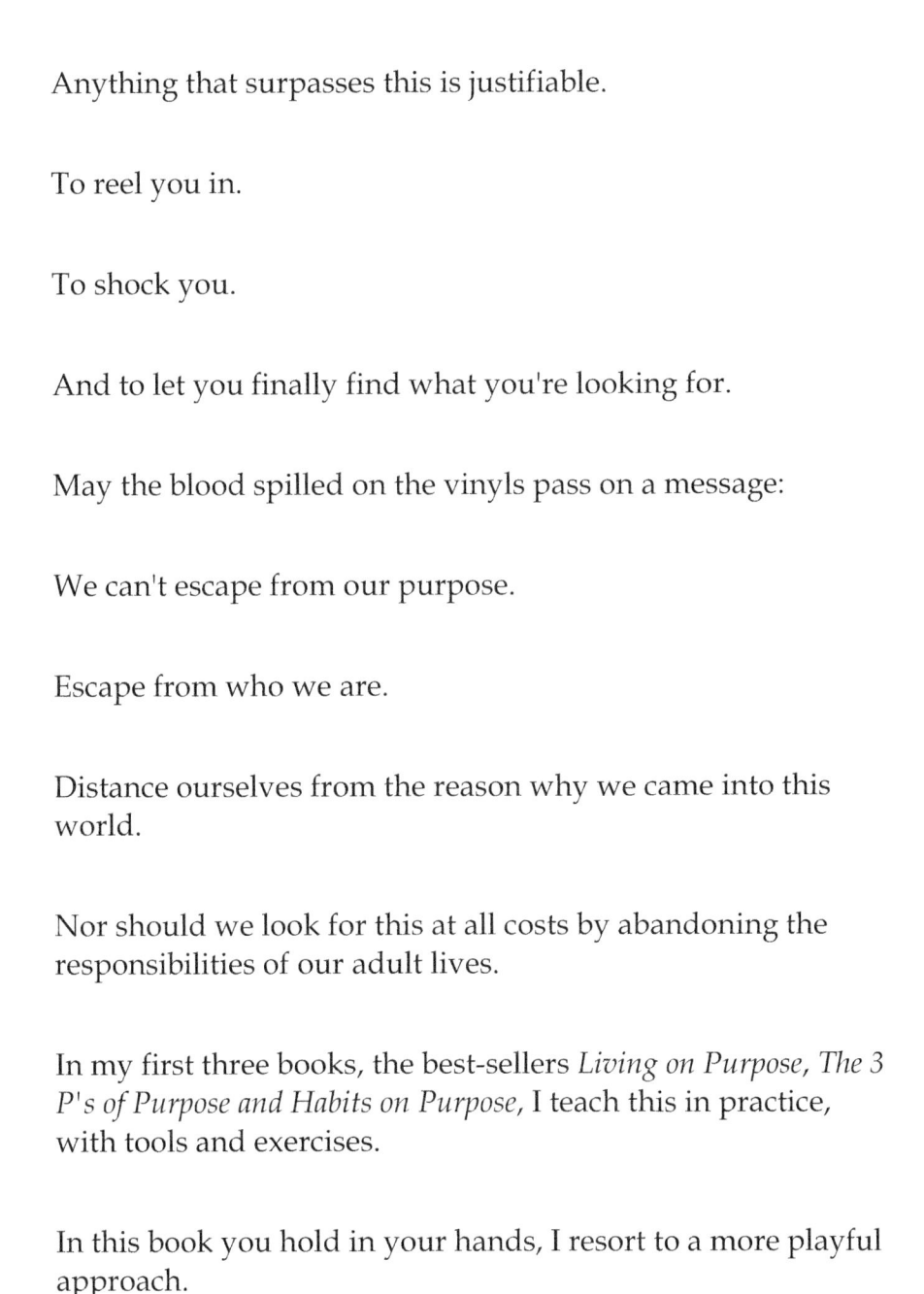

To reel you in.

To shock you.

And to let you finally find what you're looking for.

May the blood spilled on the vinyls pass on a message:

We can't escape from our purpose.

Escape from who we are.

Distance ourselves from the reason why we came into this world.

Nor should we look for this at all costs by abandoning the responsibilities of our adult lives.

In my first three books, the best-sellers *Living on Purpose*, *The 3 P's of Purpose and Habits on Purpose*, I teach this in practice, with tools and exercises.

In this book you hold in your hands, I resort to a more playful approach.

So that you, the reader, may reconnect with your very essence.

Throughout the pages, I hope you found a piece of yourself in David June.

I hope that you could relate to the feeling of anguish he carried when he was trying to escape his own fate.

I hope that you noticed how his powers awakened when he found a greater purpose in living.

May all the mystery and suspense inspire you to follow your own path.

And may no death be necessary for you to finally live.

You are David, a hero.

But you are also James, a killer…of your dreams.

That's enough of that.

DJ's purpose is to save lives through music.

That is the great contribution he wants to make to the world.

What's yours?

What can you do to help the people and the universe around you?

How can you leave your mark, your legacy?

May this book help you find the answer.

And when you come face to face with it, be the protagonist of your own path.

So, who knows, after writing self-help books and fiction, I could have the honour of writing a biography.

Yours.

Dear Reader,

As we close the chapter on "The Rythm of Death," I want to extend my deepest thanks for joining me on this journey. Your decision to dive into this story means the world to me, particularly as an independent author navigating the expansive literary seas without the support of major publishers.

If this book has touched you in any way, I kindly ask that you consider spending a minute to leave a review on Amazon. Every review truly makes a difference, helping to reach and inspire more readers like you. Your feedback is crucial for the success of this book and my ongoing journey as a writer.

Thank you again for your invaluable support. I hope we have many more stories to share in the future.

With gratitude,

Arnaldo Neto.